“LOST MEETS PL

BOOK TWO of t

by Chris Chapman

## CHAPTER ONE
## "DISCOVERY"

"You would use a bulldozer to find a China Cup!" Brody yelled angrily at Bridie, his colleague and girlfriend.

"I wish you'd stop quoting Raiders of the Lost Ark at me!" Bridie retaliated. "I can't believe that film was the reason you wanted to become an archaeologist."

"Oh, yeah! It's no better than your reason for wanting to become an archaeologist!"

Bridie paused and smiled. "Lara Croft is a much better role model then Indiana Jones!" she argued.

"Quit it, you too," demanded Doctor Condy Gill who was sitting on a fold-up chair watching the regular spectacle of the two dating scientists childishly fighting. "Apart from anything else, you both ended up as palaeontologists, not archaeologists. You are as bad as each other."

"That's rich from the doctor who became a doctor because of Doctor Who!"

"That is not true!" Condy denied insistently. "I wanted to become a timelord because of Doctor Who. I settled for being a doctor."

"I'm just so bored, Brody," Bridie went on. "I'm bored by the fact that you have to do everything so meticulously. You drag everything out until it's no fun."

Brody took a break from dusting debris from the as-yet unidentified bones they had spent weeks excavating from the soil. "There are processes,

Bridie, that have to be observed. We don't want any of these discoveries to be damaged, do we?"

As Brody was saying this, Bridie rashly and angrily climbed up into the cab of a nearby digger which had been sitting dormant for about three weeks. "Out of the way, Brody. I'm taking over this dig!"

Brody got to his feet and pointed an accusing finger at Bridie. "Come down from there. Don't do something you'll regret!"

"You know why we call it a dig, right?" Bridie asked. "It's because we dig! It isn't called a 'brush' or a 'spend weeks moving pebbles about'!" Bridie screamed while she switched on the digger's engine. "It's called a dig! So, let's dig!"

As the digger's engine roared to life, Brody put himself in front of it. "Bridie, stop being irrational, please. The remains we are finding here are beyond value for our research. These are bones of creatures we have never discovered before. It would be sacrilege to damage them."

Bridie eyed her man with girlfriend fury and shifted the digger's claw downwards sharply but briefly. "That's right, Brody. This thing can break bones, so I would move out of the way if I were you."

Brody stood his ground… for about thirty seconds, until he recognised the determination in Bridie's eyes. He had seen it many times before. Brody reluctantly stepped aside, quietly and calmly, hoping that his rationality might inspire some in her. It didn't. Brody and Condy watched in awe as Bridie ploughed the teeth of the digger into the sandy soil and pushed the claw's mouth deep into the ground.

The bones of various unknown creatures shattered and scattered and fractured. Brody and Condy screamed at Bridie to stop. Bridie lifted the digger's bucket back out of the ground, carrying with it a salad of earth, sand, weeds and crushed bones.

"Please stop it now," Brody begged.

Bridie flashed him a smile that chilled his soul.

"Bridie, we talked about this," said Condy. "Remember, count slowly to ten…"

"Ten!" Bridie screamed and she proceeded to manipulate the digger's hydraulic arm downwards into the soil again. The bucket's teeth penetrated the surface and worked its way deeper into the ground than its first visit. It quickly came to a stop accompanied by a metallic bang. Everybody froze at the unexpected sound.

"What was that?" Condy asked.

Nobody knew. Brody decided to make an uncharacteristic decision. "Bridie, keep going. Let's see what that was."

"Seriously? You don't want to take two weeks to slowly excavate the thing?"

Brody gave it some thought. "That was a distinctly metallic sound. There shouldn't be anything metal buried here. Let's find out what it is."

Half an hour later, the three explorers found themselves staring at a large metal box resting on the desert floor. The box was completely sealed. They could see no evidence of a hinge or a door or a way in of any kind. The box was clearly light enough for it not to be solid metal and when Brody knocked his fist on it, there was an echo indicating space inside. Despite being buried in the sandy soil for what could have been millions of years, the metal box shone brightly in the afternoon sun.

"We should take this back to England and have the team work on it," Brody decided.

"Or we could cut through the metal with a circular saw and find out what's inside," Bridie said.

Brody sighed. "Bridie, I've had enough of your rash impulses for today. This is my call."

"If it wasn't for my rash impulses, we might never have found this thing."

"Where do you think it comes from?" Condy asked, trying to distract them from another tiff. "I mean, how long has it been here?"

Brody looked around the site expecting something he saw to inspire the correct answer. "It's hard to tell. The only reason we're here is because the recent earthquake shifted the contents of the earth closer to the surface, so dating them is difficult."

"Just like dating you," Bridie quipped sourly.

"But the fact that the box was among these bones implies it's been here for hundreds of millions of years."

"But it's made of metal," Condy said. "Metal wasn't being manufactured into box-shapes hundreds of millions of years ago."

"The use of metal dates back to around 4000 BC," Bridie stated.

"I know," Brody admitted. "That's why it's important that we tackle this as carefully, as scientifically and as delicately as possible."

"I'll get the circular saw," Bridie decided.

Another half an hour later, Brody had completely failed to persuade his girlfriend colleague to give in to his cool scientific approach to the discovery. Bridie ripped into the metal box with the circular saw and with glee. The metal was relatively thin but incredibly robust and it took Bridie some determination to make an impact on it. Bridie had plenty of determination in this task as she was fuelled by the desire to piss off her other half. Brody watched with horror as the metal eventually gave in to the rapid revolutions of the electric saw. The box was large and rectangular, and it reminded Brody of the obelisk from 2001: A Space Odyssey (although it was silver rather than black). It occurred to his imagination, rather than his reason, that the object might have a similar alien original to the obelisk in the movie. When they had removed the box from the soil, they had laid it on its back rather than on its end, even though they had found it upright in the ground. Bridie finished cutting a rudimentary door in the front of the silver oblong, or to give it its correct three-dimensional description, the silver rectangular parallelepiped. She left a small connection intact to prevent the door she had fashioned from falling inside the box and potentially crushing whatever it contained.

"We shouldn't be doing this," Brody said for the fifth time. "There could be deadly bacteria in there for all we know."

"Why didn't you mention that before?" Condy asked in fear, covering her mouth with her coat.

"You're the doctor, Condy. It should have occurred to you before me."

Bridie sighed. "Brody, do you *really* think whoever made this box filled it up with some airborne disease?" she asked sarcastically.

"Don't patronise me like that, Bridie. The fact that this thing exists is too baffling to have any reasonable idea about what the hell it is, or what's inside it."

Bridie put down the circular saw and kneeled down next to the box. "Help me bend this back," she asked of him, taking hold of the section she had cut.

Brody gave in to her, as always, and bent down to assist her in heaving open the panel she had made. The troubled couple pulled on Bridie's improvised door and had some success at lifting it open. It wasn't until Condy reluctantly joined them that they managed to bend it sufficiently enough to reveal what was inside. Once the contents were revealed, they all stood up and stared in abject shock at what they beheld. For several moments, none of them knew how to comprehend what they were gawping at, or what to say about it. Brody eventually broke the silence.

"It's a woman!"

Bridie nodded with a smirk. "Well done, Professor, it is a woman."

"It's a naked woman!"

"You say she's been buried down there for hundreds of millions of years?" Condy asked.

"It's my best estimate."

"She's immaculate," Condy observed. "I mean, look how well preserved she is. She almost looks alive."

The woman in the box was, indeed, in excellent condition. She had the appearance of a modern woman sleeping and her structural make-up was akin to a twenty-first century human female.

"This is a game changer," Brody stuttered. "This is so 'out there' I can't even begin to understand how she exists."

"It's a prank," Bridie supposed. "Someone must have buried her here in the night or something. Maybe it's a David Blaine style magic trick."

Brody laughed at Bridie's suggestion while simultaneously considering it was probably the most realistic conclusion. "But why would anybody bury a corpse in a metal box for a magic trick?"

"Maybe she's not a corpse," Bridie suggested. "We should check her pulse."

"There is no way anybody could survive being encased in a sealed metal box under the ground, even for ten minutes, never mind for at least the number of hours we've been on the site today."

"Go on. Check her pulse. Let's be sure."

Brody stared at his girlfriend, and a million confused thoughts scampered around in his mind. While he hesitated, Condy decided to take action, and she knelt down next to the metal coffin putting her hand on the woman's wrist to test for a pulse.

"Condy, don't be ridiculous. Whether this is a genuine find or a prank, in either case, it isn't possible for this woman to be alive."

Condy moved her hand from the woman's wrist to her neck in order to check for the carotid pulse.

"You see!" Brody exclaimed. "If you can't feel a pulse in the wrist, you're not going to feel it in her neck."

"There's a pulse," Condy revealed nervously. "It's weak, but there is a definite pulse."

Brody shook his head dismissively. "No. You can just feel your own pulse in your fingers. It's a common mistake."

"I'm a qualified physician, Brody," Condy retaliated simply. "Feel it for yourself."

Brody stamped on his feelings of conspiracy from the two girls and knelt down to feel for a pulse, determined to prove them wrong. He put his fingertips to the woman's neck and was immediately staggered by the sensation that he could feel a rhythmic beat that was too slow to be the pulse of his own heart rate. He held his fingers there for an extended period while the enormity of what had occurred over the past few minutes shrouded him.

"Okay," he said, attempting to get on his feet again, but instead falling on his backside. "Okay. Okay," he repeated. "Let's get her back to HQ."

A few hours later, Brody, Condy and Bridie were back at their headquarters. The woman they had found in the metal box was prone on an operating table, covered by a surgical blanket. Also present in the room were Zachary Johannessen and Karen LaGrance, the two business partners who were sponsoring the excavation, and two of Condy's assistant nurses. Zachary was an eccentric but likeable millionaire who amused himself by investing in crackpot schemes and unsupportable projects. His interest in this dig was peaked when he was approached by palaeontologist Brody Hollohan who claimed he had scientific evidence that something historically anomalous existed in this particular region of North America and that the earthquake had given them the perfect advantage to explore what could potentially be the find of the century. However, Brody had neglected to explain that the scientific evidence he was speaking of was a dream he'd had. Thankfully, Zachary hadn't asked to see the evidence.

Karen LaGrance had got involved when she heard through her network of industrial spies that Zachary was onto something potentially world changing. Mrs. LaGrance was ambitious, paranoid, megalomaniacal, greedy, sociopathic and power-mad. She had offered her own investment coupled with the threat that if they didn't accept her as a business partner, she would expose their discovery to the rest of the world. Brody took her money, happily, knowing that the real threat was that if she told the world what Brody said he had, the world would have exposed him as being a dreamer rather than a scientist, and he would lose all investments.

"We have done all the tests that are available to us at the camp," Condy was telling the group. "Erm, she appears to be human but… there are differences."

"Differences?" Mrs. LaGrance asked.

"Yes, her internal organs, according to the scans, are exactly the same as ours, but in stupendously good condition. However, when we tried to take a blood sample, we were unable to pierce the skin. We tried several needles and they all broke."

Condy took a syringe and pressed it against the woman's arm to demonstrate. The needle easily snapped.

"So, we tried something stronger."

Condy then picked up a scalpel and pressed it to the woman's arm. After a few seconds of pressure from Condy, the scalpel blade began to bend. Condy raised the scalpel to show the group how much it had been bent. Gawps of awe rippled around the room like a Mexican wave.

"So, we tried something stronger."

Condy next took a large butcher's knife from her tray of instruments. Brody, Bridie, and Zachary all gasped. Mrs. LaGrance flashed a wicked, sinister grin. Condy raised the knife into the air and plummeted it into the woman's arm. Actually, the knife didn't go *into* her arm at all. The blade simply bounced off, giving a sort of thud that sounded like punching meat with an iron fist. Everybody stared awe-struck.

"What does it mean?" Zachary asked. "Is she a superhero? Or did they do something to her skin during the preservation process?"

"Preservation process?" Condy asked him.

"Yes, the metal box is obviously some kind of coffin, isn't it?" Zachary supposed in the form of a question. "And they did something to her skin to strengthen it… for preservation?"

Zachary looked around the room wondering why everybody was staring at him like he was a lunatic. He decided to make another suggestion. "Or maybe she's an alien and the metal box is her spaceship."

Brody made the decision to speak. "Zachary, the reason we're all looking at you like you've just farted is that this woman isn't dead. She has a pulse."

"She what?" Zachary screamed.

"She what?" Mrs. LaGrance cried.

"Oh," Bridie exclaimed. "Now I see what has happened. Nobody told either of you that she was alive."

"But I thought you said she'd been buried under the ground for thousands of billions of years?"

"Millions."

"Well, fine, whatever, still a very, very long time."

"I assumed you'd told them that she was still alive," Condy said to Brody.

"I figured the medical team would have taken care of that."

"Boys and girls, stop quibbling," Mrs. LaGrance commanded. "Tell me what you know."

Nobody said anything at first. Condy realised they were all waiting for her to say something. "She has a pulse, but it's very slow. It's like she's in a coma. Actually, it's more like… it's more like she's in hibernation."

This was followed by a silence which told everybody that what Condy had said so far was the extent of what they knew about the mystery woman.

"Can we wake her up?" Zachary asked optimistically.

Condy fiddled with her glasses and took in a deep breath. "There are several things we could try, but we don't know enough about her physiology to know if anything will be effective or if we might hurt her."

"She has impenetrable skin," Mrs. LaGrance coldly stated. "I get the feeling we would have a hard task damaging her."

"Then maybe it's not a good idea to wake her. She might be hostile," Brody suggested.

Some members of the party nodded agreement.

"Don't be such a wuss, Brody," Mrs. LaGrance chided. "What do we try first?"

Condy gave it some thought. "We might as well start with smelling salts, and if that doesn't work, we'll move onto something stronger."

"Like Brody's socks," Bridie joked. Only Condy laughed.

"Fetch the smelling salts," Mrs. LaGrance insisted.

Condy instructed one of her nurses to fetch the smelling salts. The nurse hurried away to the supply cabinet. After some frantic searching, the nurse returned.

"I can't find the smelling salts, doctor," the nurse revealed.

Condy went over to the supply cabinet herself to check for the smelling salts. She scoured the cabinet thoroughly. "Apparently, we have no smelling salts," she told the group.

"Fetch Brody's socks!" Zachary playfully suggested.

Everybody turned to look at Brody.

"You're joking, right?" said Brody.

"Actually I was, but…"

"Brody, at the end of a working day, your feet smell like bins," Bridie revealed to the room. A number of people laughed.

"Let's give it a try," Condy suggested with a smirk on her face.

Brody shook his head. "Condy, you're a scientist. Are you seriously suggesting we use smelling socks to revive her?"

"In the absence of an alternative… I've smelt your feet, Brody. They're rank."

Brody couldn't believe it. He even looked to Mrs. LaGrance for a voice of reason. Mrs. LaGrance was difficult and headstrong and unconscionable, but at the very least, she had a level-headed approach to problem solving. On this occasion, however, she seemed willing to try anything. It was in an attempt to demonstrate to everyone how ridiculous their suggestion was, that Brody decided to remove one of his socks and hand it to Condy. Condy took the sock, bearing a revulsive expression, and deliberately holding it at arm's length.

"Maybe we should get your bodyguard in here," Condy said to Mrs. LaGrance. "In case she does wake up. We aught to be careful."

Mrs. LaGrance called her personal bodyguard on her phone and he arrived within minutes. His name was Edmund. He was well built, short and reasonably unattractive. He stood dutifully beside Mrs. LaGrance.

"Here goes," Condy said dramatically, and she proceeded to hover Brody's sock just beneath the mystery woman's nose.

Within seconds, the mystery woman coughed and sat upright. Condy screamed in surprise and staggered backwards, slamming into the desk behind her. The woman darted her eyes around the room, startled and confused. Everybody else in the room took a couple of steps backwards and gaped incredulously at the woman, holding their hands out in front of them as if to defend themselves from a potential attack. The woman did nothing for a few eternal seconds before she lunged at Bridie, who was closest to her, placing her hands on the young girl's throat and pushing her temple against Bridie's. Mrs. LaGrance's bodyguard flew into action and he tried to pull the woman away from the terrified Bridie. The woman was incredibly strong, and Edmund was having difficulty moving her. This difficulty was compounded by the fact that he was nervous about where to place his hands on the naked woman. The woman barely flinched before effortlessly casting the bodyguard across the room, through a closed door into the adjoining room. Edmund didn't return from the adjoining room after that. Despite their relationship problems, Brody felt compelled to leap to Bridie's rescue and he grabbed one of Bridie's arms in an attempt to pull her away from the aggression of the mystery woman. Each time he pulled at her, Bridie screamed as if he was causing her pain. Eventually, he eased on the pulling, but held firmly onto her arm.

"Bridie, I've got you. It's going to be okay," he tried to reassure her.

Bridie didn't, or couldn't, respond. Her eyes were fixed on the mystery woman's eyes. The mystery woman continued to press her forehead oppressively at Bridie's, until she quickly let go of the girl altogether, and Bridie fell into Brody's arms.

The mystery woman stood before them. Her confusion had turned to confidence and everybody felt belittled by her presence.

"My name is Julianne," she said to them. "And I need your help."

# CHAPTER TWO
# "MYSTERY WOMAN"

"I have co-ordinates to my home. I need you to take me there," Julianne said.

"Wait. We have a couple of questions first. Who are you?" Brody asked. "And what did you do to Bridie?"

Bridie had been unresponsive since her encounter with Julianne. She was sitting on the floor with her head in her hands, refusing to speak to anybody, but she seemed unharmed.

"I didn't intend to hurt the girl. I needed to access her memory so that I could understand your language."

"You read her mind?" Brody asked accusingly.

"I looked at the surface to perceive an understanding of the language you use, but I didn't invade her thoughts or personal feelings. A comparable perspective would be like the difference between reading a book and knowing the author."

Everybody thought they understood but they were still suspicious of the mystery woman.

"Am I making sense?" Julianne asked. "I am struggling to express my meaning. Your language is so primate."

"You mean primitive," Brody corrected ironically.

Julianne threw Brody a dismissive yet understanding look. "Perhaps I underestimate the complexities of your lingual flexibility," she modestly supposed. "Your mode of speech is new to me."

"Who are you?" Zachary asked, feeling that the question hadn't been adequately answered. He was also in awe of her nakedness. "And can I buy you a drink?"

Julianne considered both questions, and she decided to ignore the second one. "I am the beginning of all knowledge that you seek."

"Jesus!" Zachary exclaimed.

"What does the son of your creator have to do with this?" Julianne asked.

"Well," Brody began. "Many English-speaking people use the name of Jesus as an exclamation."

Julianne looked confused. "You use your religious idols as profanity?" she asked incredulously. "I don't understand the correlation."

Brody rubbed his eyes. "Oh, God!" he said.

"Oh, God?" Julianne asked.

"Never mind."

Julianne paused and tilted her head as though she was accessing her memory. "God is your name for the creator of your species."

"That's right," Condy confirmed.

"And you use his name as profanity as well?" Julianne asked.

"I guess we do," said Brody.

"You people have no idea about the origin of your species," Julianne surmised. "No wonder you use your religious figures as swear words. It's because you know that they are false. I can show you the truth of your birth. Take me to my home and I will reveal to you the fact of your provenance."

"Would you like me to get you a robe first?" Condy sweetly asked. "You must be… chilly."

"No, thank you," Julianne replied.

"No, she doesn't need a robe!" Zachary eagerly echoed.

"She's fine as she is," concurred Brody.

"It's the Bermuda Triangle," Bridie exclaimed after Julianne had given them the coordinates to the place she called home.

"The Bermuda Triangle?" Julianne asked.

"It's an area near a place called Bermuda where it has been reported that many ships and aircraft have mysteriously vanished since the 1950s, and many people have supposed that the place is supernatural."

Julianne nodded. "Supernatural is the right word. It is where all life began, and it began with me."

"That's quite a claim," said Mrs. LaGrance.

"I suppose that makes you Eve, does it?" Condy asked sarcastically. Condy's parents were devout Christians and even though Condy, as a scientist, was sceptical of God, she still had respect for and a certain amount of belief in the religion.

"Eve?" Julianne asked.

"According to many religious beliefs, Eve was the very first woman," Brody explained.

"Do you use her name as profanity as well?"

"Actually, no."

"Well, I'm not Eve. I wasn't the first woman."

"That's more like it," Mrs. LaGrance said. "You've finally said something I can believe."

"I was the second woman."

This claim from Julianne caused a silence which nobody knew how to break.

"So, just how long have you been in that metal box?" Brody asked. "And why were you in there in the first place?"

"Your questions will be answered in time," Julianne replied. "How long will it take us to get to this Bermuda Triangle?"

"I don't know about anybody else but I'm not exactly happy about the idea of just sailing into the Bermuda Triangle at this woman's whim," Condy said.

Nobody else said anything.

"Brody?" Condy asked, expecting his advocacy.

"We came here to make a discovery, and Julianne is offering to show us the origin of the species. How can we turn it down?"

"I'm game," Bridie concurred. "Even though she attacked me. You all know me, anything for adventure."

The two nurses in the room stayed silent even though they secretly agreed with Condy that they shouldn't go.

"Hell, I've been all over the world, but never visited Bermuda. Why not?" Zachary exclaimed.

"I don't believe you people," Condy moaned, shaking her head.

"I always operate with caution, tactics, planning…" Mrs. LaGrance began, "However, if there is any truth in what this woman is saying, this could be worth a fortune. We'd be fools not to endeavour."

"Aren't you rich enough?" Condy asked her.

"Silly question, silly girl."

Condy removed her spectacles and let them clatter on the desk in front of her. She had no reason to do this, other than to make a dramatic gesture. "Well, you can't make me go!"

"No," Brody replied. "But I can ask you to. We need a doctor, and you're the only one we have on the expedition. You're also the only doctor I trust."

Condy looked sternly at Brody with an expression which said, 'don't con me'.

"We need you with us. And think about it, Condy. I've known you long enough to know that you have confused and ambiguous feelings towards religion. If Julianne is telling the truth, this is our opportunity to find out the absolute facts of the meaning of life. Isn't that possibility worth a tiny bit of risk?"

Condy smiled tiredly at Brody and decided to reply with a film quote because she knew he loved movies. "You had me at hello."

Brody laughed. "I didn't even say hello," he replied.

Condy chuckled. "You know what I mean."

"Brilliant!"

Everybody gathered around and discussed their plan of action. Julianne wandered outside into the warm afternoon sun and basked in her recent freedom. After the group discussion was finished, everybody set about their immediate tasks. Zachary and Mrs. LaGrance gathered the captain of Mrs. LaGrance's ship which had brought them all to the expedition, and the two millionaires explained the situation and revealed their intended destination. There was unrest and scepticism from a lot of the crew, but they were loyal to Mrs. LaGrance because she was truly terrifying, and they kept their grievances largely to themselves.

Condy saw Julianne standing in the sun with her head tilted upwards and her eyes closed, and she decided to approach her. Even to Condy who was strictly hetero, the sight of Julianne's naked body bathed in sunlight was stunning.

"Are you human, Julianne?" she asked directly.

Julianne smiled at the question. "No, but I was created by the same… deity as you."

"And that's what we are going to find at those coordinates in Bermuda?"

"Yes. There is an island at the centre of what you call the Bermuda Triangle, and it is protected from the outside world. That is why so many ships and aircraft have vanished there."

Condy absorbed this information. "So how do we know that we won't vanish as well?"

"I'm hoping that we will vanish," Julianne said. "That's how we get to the island."

Condy sighed. "I think I'm going to stop asking questions now."

"Do you believe the things that I say?"

"Well, if you were just a normal person saying these things, I would think you were crazy. But we found you completely sealed in a metal box. There's no way that you could breathe in there…"

"Breathe?"

"And the fact that your skin seems all but impenetrable, means that anything you say is potentially true."

Julianne started to laugh as a realisation struck her. "I'm sorry, I completely forgot that you are only mortals."

Condy stared at Julianne. "Oh, you're an immortal," she replied with deliberate cool. "I should have realised."

"I am one of five immortals. The four others should still be on the island"

"And the island, does it have a name?"

"We call it Mesaglenedendeltor."

Condy raised her eyebrows at the mouthful. "Mesa…?"

"Mesaglenedendeltor," Julianne repeated.

"How do you spell that?" Condy asked, slightly humorously.

"Exactly as it sounds."

Condy decided to dig a little further. "And the other four 'immortals', who are they?"

"Are we ready to leave yet?" Julianne interrupted, abruptly.

"Erm… just about. The crew are getting prepared now."

On the ship, the captain was organising the crew to prepare for their voyage. The captain was reluctant and confused about the purpose or the necessity of the journey, but he was loyal to Mrs.

LaGrance. In their cabin, Brody and Bridie were unpacking some of their personal items they had brought from their base on-land.

"Are you alright?" Brody asked his girlfriend with a slightly distant, almost automatic tone.

"You mean after that super-strong mystery woman had me so tightly by the throat that I almost choked? Yes, I'm peachy."

"Why are you always sarcastic with me these days?"

"Because you're so cold towards me. Even when you're acting concerned, you're only *acting* concerned."

Brody sighed. His relationship with Bridie had deteriorated rapidly in the last couple of months. They had been friends and colleagues for many years, and it had only been six months since they had decided to try being a couple. It was a decision borne of circumstance and logic rather than passion. They both knew that it had been a mistake, but neither was willing to address the issue in case it affected their working relationship or their long-term friendship. The key result of their reluctance to face the music was that they had become increasingly distant and acerbic towards each other. The situation had become so desperate that Bridie had proposed to Brody, mistakenly thinking that making the ultimate commitment to each other might have solved their problems. Brody had sensibly suggested it wasn't a good idea which had only made their relationship worse.

"We should have just stayed friends," Brody blurted.

Bridie sighed with sorry relief. "Finally, one of us had the guts to say it," she expressed. "It's been on my mind for weeks. We really made a mess of things between us."

"It was a mistake."

"Do you think so?" Bridie contrarily asked. Brody felt like he was in trouble now. "You're saying being with me is a mistake?"

"No, no, that's not what I mean. Being with you would be great for anybody. But me and you are simply much better as friends than we are as lovers."

Bridie nodded. "Yes. I think, in the beginning, the sex was really…"

"Awkward!" Brody exclaimed.

Bridie hesitated. "I was going to say great."

"Oh, shit!"

"You thought it was awkward?"

"Don't get upset. I just meant that when you're friends with someone for a long time and there are established, mutual boundaries, it can be a bit confusing when those boundaries are broken. The first time I saw you naked, it felt deeply forbidden like there was a hidden part of you that wasn't my business and I was suddenly exposed to it."

Bridie's face was difficult for Brody to read, despite how well he knew her. "I think I know what you mean. The first time I saw your… man-toy, it was almost like you'd been keeping it secret from me and finding out that you had one made me feel like my best friend had betrayed me. Does that sound weird?"

"Yes, it does," Brody stated facetiously. They both laughed.

"So, what do you say?" Bridie asked. "Just friends?"

"Are we splitting up?"

Bridie smiled. "Yes. I think it's the only way to fix things between us."

"Wow. It feels good."

"We should never have got together."

"Well, I don't know about that," Brody suggested. "Maybe it was something we had to get out of the way. At least now we know it doesn't work."

Bridie put her arms around Brody and they hugged with a platonic passion which was the closest they had felt towards each other for a long time.

"Can I ask you something?" Bridie said after the hug.

"Yes."

"And you'll be honest?"

Brody nodded. "Now that we aren't a couple, I can be honest with you."

Bridie laughed even though she knew it hadn't been a joke.

"What was the real reason you didn't want to marry me?"

Brody sighed, but proceeded with honesty. "It wasn't that I didn't want to marry *you*, specifically, I just have a real problem with the institution of marriage. My parents were unhappily married for years before they finally got a divorce and got their lives back. I realised a long time ago that I'm just not the marrying kind."

Bridie gave him a small smile. "So, it wasn't that you didn't love me?"

"I do love you. I'll always love you, Bridie, but platonically."

Bridie's smile got a little bigger. Her eyes moistened just a little. "I love you, too... platonically."

"But just because we're platonic," Brody went on half seriously, "doesn't mean I don't reserve the right to be jealous of all future boyfriends."

Bridie laughed. "Oh, you know I'm gonna be jealous of every girl you even just talk to."

"So, now we're not a couple, are you going to stop being mean to me all time?"

"Of course not. Just because you're not my boyfriend anymore, doesn't mean I'm not the boss."

Brody sighed lightly and grinned at his friend. "Yes, Ma'am."

While Brody and Bridie executed their amicable irreconciliation, the two real bosses of the organisation, Zachary Johannessen and Mrs. Karen LaGrance were boarding the ship with the help of their four-person entourage. The entourage scuttled Zachary and Mrs. LaGrance's belongings into their cabins while the two masters of industry waited for the captain to arrive on the bridge. Zachary seemed unusually jittery.

"Are you sure we're doing the right thing?" he asked his colleague eventually.

"Why are you here?"

"What do you mean?" Zachary responded in confusion.

"You have a reputation for being an eccentric millionaire. All your ex-wives have said that your marriages always fail because you're too focussed on your business. And yet, with this project, you seem reluctant to get stuck in or take any risks. So, why are you here?"

"I invest in small businesses and unique projects in order to give talented people a chance to make something for themselves, but that woman we just found," Zachary said, pausing for effect. "She isn't small business. She's either an outstandingly elaborate con, or she's literally a goddess. Either way, I'm not sure it makes good business sense."

"How did you get to your position, being such a coward?"

Zachary sighed. "It's not cowardice, it's caution. I got to my position by making sensible big decisions and risky small ones. The combination of the two has worked for me very well."

"I knew I should have met you before agreeing to work with you. I based my decision on your eccentric reputation. I had no idea you were going to be so… reasonable," Mrs. LaGrance moaned.

Zachary laughed. "Is there something wrong with being reasonable?"

"Yes, when you're facing things which are beyond reason," she asserted. "And like you said, whether this Julianne is a con artist or a goddess, the situation is clearly beyond reason."

It was at this point in the conversation that the captain came to the bridge with a selection of his crew. They all discussed their reservations about the trip to the Bermuda Triangle and how reckless it was for them to be expected to put their lives in such danger. Their objections were soon quashed with the offer of more money for everyone.

In her cabin, Condy was on her mobile phone, attempting to call her boyfriend. The call went to voicemail and Condy left him the following message.

"Hey, hon. Listen, I was hoping to speak to you in person but I guess you're... Look, there's no easy way to tell you this but I'm going to the Bermuda Triangle with an immortal woman we found buried in the sand, in the hope that, if we survive the journey, we might discover a lost island which contains all the secrets of the universe..." Condy paused to think if she had left anything out. "Try not to worry and don't forget to feed the parrot. Love you. Bye. Call me back. Bye."

Shortly after this, the main crew and personnel involved in what was now being slightly sarcastically called the Genesis Project, were aboard their ship and setting sail for Bermuda.

# CHAPTER TWO
# "VOYAGE"

It was dinner time. Eating together at the captain's table were Zachary, Mrs. LaGrance, Brody, Bridie, Condy, Edmund, and the company psychiatrist, Iain. Julianne hadn't been asked to join them for the time-being. She had agreed to remain in her quarters with two guards posted outside her door. She could easily overpower two men, but she wanted to put everyone to as much ease as she could. The captain, on this occasion, was not at the captain's table, but on the bridge supervising the journey.

"My worry is her psychological health," the psychiatrist was saying about Julianne. "If she was buried in a metal box and left alone for millions of years, surely she would have gone cu… cu… cuckoo."

Condy swallowed the Yorkshire pudding she had been chewing. "I think it's reasonable to assume she has been in hibernation for most of that time."

"Hibernation?" the psychiatrist asked, sceptically.

"Yes, she was in some kind of torpor when we discovered her. According to Julianne, it was self-induced."

"Does she have any idea how long she was buried?" Zachary asked.

"No. She said it was possible it was millions of years, but it could have been twenty minutes for all she could tell."

"Do you believe she is really immortal?" Mrs. LaGrance asked.

Condy considered the question carefully. "I believe she is incredibly strong. She demonstrated preternatural strength, and her skin is virtually impermeable, if not *actually* impermeable."

"So, she's a superhero!" Brody facetiously supposed.

"That's what I said earlier," Zachary cooed.

"Personally, I think she's a god," Condy said, quite seriously.

"Maybe it's you that's cu… cu… cuckoo," the psychiatrist zinged.

"Iain!" Mrs. LaGrance chided the psychiatrist. "I need you, of all people, to take this matter seriously, if you would."

Iain said nothing, but slightly nodded.

"Although, I do tend to agree with him," Mrs. LaGrance said with uncharacteristic contrariness. "Thinking she's a god is cuckoo."

"Listen," Condy replied, mounting her defence, "I'm a scientist and I was brought up in a religious environment. I have been equally exposed to creationism and evolutionism, and in considering both of those perspectives, coupled with the discovery of Julianne, I believe it is our scientific duty to approach this unique project with an open mind. And when I open my mind, it makes logical sense to consider that the powerful woman we have met today could be what we would refer to as a god. Not *the* God, but a god."

Everybody absorbed what Condy had to say, and none of them could dispute her rationality, considering the evidence before them.

"Okay," Bridie said on behalf of the group.

After this they all concentrated on their food for a while and eventually the conversation moved on to other things.

"So, Brody," Zachary said, "If you could choose a superpower, what would it be?"

Brody laughed. He always liked this game. "I would be fast," he replied. "Flying is kind of cool, but I always just wanted to be really fast, like The Flash!"

"What would your name be?"

"Brody," said Brody simply.

"You know what I mean. You'd need a superhero name."

"I'd just be me. I wouldn't hide behind a name. I think that's just cowardly."

"Oh, come on, Brody," Condy chipped in. "Every superhero has an alter ego."

"That's right, to protect the people you love," Zachary agreed.

"You wouldn't want tu… tu… to expose yourself," Iain, the psychiatrist advised.

Brody sighed because he couldn't think of a name. "I don't know. Maybe I'd just be The Flash."

"You can't be The Flash, it's taken."

"How about The Flasher?" Bridie joked.

"I thought you didn't want me to expose myself."

The whole table laughed.

"I like the superhero names that end in 'o', like Magneto and Pyro," Brody suggested.

"So, you could be Fasto or something like that?" Zachary said.

"I've got it," Bridie piped up. "Speedo!"

The whole table laughed again.

"I like that," Brody said. "And what about you, Zachary, what would your superpower be?"

Zachary sat back with glee on his face. "I always wanted to be Batman. He's the coolest of all the superheroes."

Brody flinched. "But he doesn't have any powers! He's just a millionaire in an expensive suit. You can choose any superpower and you're choosing a suit?"

"Chicks would dig me."

"But that's stupid," Brody went on. "Why not choose a superpower and then have the suit as well. You could be Batman-plus-one. Batman with a superpower."

Zachary realised Brody was right. "Okay," he said, and he sipped from his glass of wine. Zachary then looked at his wine for inspiration. "I'd be The Intoxicator! I would make people too drunk to stand just by breathing on them."

"That's inspired!"

"I'll drink to that."

Everyone took a drink. "Cheers."

"I'd want to predict the future," Iain suggested as his superpower.

Everyone else went silent thinking it was a pretty lame idea.

"That's a pretty lame idea," Zachary observed.

"And that just demonstrates what a great power it would be!" Iain claimed. "If I'd bu… bu… been able to predict that you would all react so badly to my idea of predicting the future, I wouldn't have said it."

Suddenly the idea seemed quite good.

"This is a silly conversation," Mrs. LaGrance said. The rest of the group, despite the fun they were having, found themselves feeling foolish. Mrs. LaGrance had a way of making people feel small. "However," she went on, "I think I would be The Dominator, and I would stand above everyone and intimidate them with my influence."

This was met with silence as they all had a similar thought. "I think you already have that power," Brody bravely suggested before he could stop himself

"Thank you."

"What about you, Bridie?"

Bridie had been thinking about it but hadn't come up with anything. "I don't know. What do you think my power would be, Brody?"

Brody gave it some thought, and the answer came to him quite quickly. "You don't need a superpower," he said. "You'd put on a costume and get stuck into the fight whether you had powers or not. Fearlessness – that's your superpower."

Bridie welled up a little bit. "I love you," she said appreciatively.

"Yeah, I love you, too."

Other people in the room were taken aback by their exchange. For the most part, everyone had only seen Brody and Bridie fighting and this was a refreshing development.

"We just broke up," Brody announced to the room. He then leaned over and took Bridie's hand, which she accepted eagerly.

Everyone was even more taken aback. "Er…" Zachary began. "Sorry to hear that, guys."

"It's alright," Bridie explained. "We realised our friendship was suffering, so we've become friends again."

"It's about time," Condy exclaimed. "It's been hell watching you two fall apart these last couple of months. I think you've made the right decision."

"So, Condy. Your superpower?" Brody asked. "You'd be a healer presumably – someone who can cure the sick and the wounded."

"Oh no, I'd want invisibility," she blurted immediately. "I can't think of anything more useful than being invisible whenever I want to be."

Brody made an 'eah' sound to indicate his indifference to Condy's answer. "Fairly boring, but practical."

"I could use it to follow my boyfriend and find out what he gets up to."

The sting of Condy's rationale for her choice of superpower resonated with many in the group. None of them had met Condy's boyfriend, but they had all spent time listening to her defend him too much. Bridie reached over and took Condy's hand. "He doesn't deserve you," she told Condy reassuringly.

"So, that just leaves Edmund," Brody said. "So, come on, Mr. Bodyguard, what would your superpower be?"

Edmund had spent the entire conversation standing guard near Mrs. LaGrance, his employer, being dutifully alert. He had his answer prepared but he was a little disappointed that somebody had said it already. "I'd have to go with invisibility as well. As a bodyguard, it would be invaluable."

A couple of people nodded, in agreement that it was a good point but a boring answer.

"And as two invisible people," Edmund continued, "maybe you and me could hook up," he concluded, looking at Condy.

Condy winced but felt bad about it. "Well, Edmund," she said. "Maybe, if you were invisible, it would be the only time we might hook up… if I didn't have to see your face."

Everyone reacted nervously to Condy's burn. Edmund took it in good humour. He walked over to one of the supply cupboards, found a large paper bag and put it over his head.

"Will this do?" he asked.

They all laughed at Edmund's confident retaliation to Condy's rejection, celebrating his nerve. Condy was especially impressed. Her boyfriend's despicable insistence to ignore her had made her susceptible to any kind of flattery. She got up from her seat, walked over to Edmund, removed the bag from his head and she kissed him on the cheek. Edmund grinned like a giddy child.

"Did I score points?" he asked her.

Condy felt herself being seduced but wasn't prepared to answer Edmund's question. She smiled at him tenderly and returned to her seat.

"Did he score points?" Brody eagerly asked on Edmund's behalf.

"Shut up," Condy said coyly.

Everyone knew that Edmund had scored points.

After their dinner, everybody retired to their quarters for the night. Brody had decided to let Bridie have the cabin that they had previously shared, and he had taken some of his personal things to one of the many empty cabins aboard Mrs. LaGrance's huge and beautiful ship. Just as he was settling down and picking a Netflix movie to watch, there was a knock at his door. He answered it and found Condy standing outside.

"Can I come in?" Condy asked.

"Sure," Brody replied, stepping aside for her to enter the room. Brody couldn't help but feel a little unsure. It seemed strangely intimate for the two of them to be in the room together. Condy was an attractive woman but there had never been any hint of anything between them, so her being in his room felt a little uncomfortable. He tried to shake it off as being silly.

"Is something the matter?" he asked in order to break the silence. She seemed hesitant to talk, but obviously had something to say.

"No," she replied quickly. "It's just that I was talking to Julianne earlier about where we are going. She wasn't giving up much information but what she did tell me was that we are going to an island called..." she tried her best to remember it, but it wouldn't come. "I've got it written down."

Condy produced a slip of paper from her pocket and read the name. "Mesaglenedendeltor."

Brody took the paper from Condy and studied it. "Should that mean something to me?"

"Perhaps not at first glance," Condy admitted, "but if you break the word down, it reveals something interesting. Now, the first part of the word, mesa, means mountain, more or less. The second part, glen, means valley, more or less. So, these words are contrary to each other. A place can't be a mountain and a valley at the same time. The same goes for the end part of the name. Del and tor mean mountain and valley. Now, if we remove these self-contradictory tautologies, what part of the word are we left with?"

Brody examined the word and did as Condy suggested, ignoring the mountain and valley parts of the island's name. "Eden," Brody replied with awestruck drama in his tone. He stared at Condy, wondering what she thought of this discovery.

Condy grinned and remained quiet at first. "I'm allowing myself the luxury of believing that we're going to the garden of Eden,"

"That's ridiculous."

"I know, but aren't you excited about the smallest possibility that it's true? That we might be on the verge of discovering something extramundane?"

Brody laughed out of sheer wonder. "Yes, I am," he admitted, still laughing, this time at himself. "Why did you come and tell me about this? Why not tell the whole group?"

"Honestly? I thought they might all think it was silly," Condy told him. "I can't quite tell how seriously everybody's taking this whole situation. I mean, yesterday afternoon we met a woman who might be a god, and in the evening we were telling each other what superpowers we would have. Either we're all in shock and avoiding the reality of what's going on, or we are being incredibly level-headed and professional about it."

"I suspect the former," Brody admitted.

"Exactly. So, until we get there, I think we should keep some of these details among the scientists. You can tell Bridie if you want."

Brody nodded in agreement and then they said goodnight to each other and Condy left the room. Brody sat on his bed and allowed his mind to reel with all the stuff that was going on. A few minutes later, there was another knock on his door. Brody got up, slightly vexed, and answered the door. On the other side was Iain, the ship's psychiatrist.

"I just thought I'd pu… pu... pop by and see how you were doing?" Iain asked.

Brody nodded calmly. "Fine, I think. I'm a little nervous about where we're going and what we'll find when we get there, but I think I'm dealing."

"Exciting times," Iain said plainly.

They stood nodding for a few moments. "What do you really want, Iain?" Brody finally asked.

"I just wanted to come and gloat about the fact that I've been telling you for months that your relationship with Bridie should be pu…pu… platonic and not romantic, and that the two of you would be happier if you could find a way to be friends again."

"Yes, I know," Brody conceded, "but I figured you were too much of a professional to knock on my door and say I told you so."

Iain smiled at Brody's comment. "The point is, you should listen to my advice more often. And tonight, my advice is that you get plenty of sleep. I have a feeling the next few days are going to be... testing!"

Brody promised he would heed Iain's words and get a good night's sleep. They said goodnight to each other and after Brody had closed his door, he binge-watched a whole series of something called Russian Doll on Netflix before falling asleep.

# CHAPTER THREE
# "ARRIVAL"

Brody awoke to the sounds of commotion. He could hear running footsteps and panicked voices. There was an eerie creaking as if the ship was struggling to do its job and there was the distinct noise of crashing waves. Brody sat up and experienced a swaying sensation as though he was drunk or hungover, but he quickly realised it was due to the rocking movement of the ship. He went over to the sink and threw some water on his face before exiting his cabin. A couple of crew members ran past him in the corridor.

"What's going on?" he asked.

"We're sinking!" one of them cried.

"We think we're sinking," the other one amended.

They both continued to run until they were out of sight. Brody decided to make his way towards the bridge of the ship. On the bridge he found the captain, some crew, Zachary, Mrs. LaGrance and Bridie.

"What's going on?" Brody asked.

They all turned to look at him.

"Where have you been?" Bridie asked crossly.

"I was up late, I couldn't sleep," he replied lamely, "and then, apparently, I couldn't wake up."

"We entered the Bermuda Triangle, against my protestations, and the weather turned inclement," the captain explained while fiddling with his instruments.

"That's an understatement," said Zachary.

"And before we knew it, we were surrounded by this thick fog," the captain continued.

Brody looked at the viewing window more closely. He had noticed the foggy screens when he had entered the bridge. "That's fog? I thought the screens were just misted over."

"No, it's fog," the captain iterated. "Go outside and check if you don't believe me, but don't expect to do any breathing while you're out there. We already have one of my crew in sick bay after he tried going outside."

Brody took the captain at his word. "I'm pretty fond of breathing, I think I'll stay here."

"Sensible."

"Are we sinking?" Brody asked. "One of the crew said he thought we were sinking."

"That's just panic. We are perfectly buoyant," the captain assured him.

"For now," Bridie added.

As if to demonstrate Bridie's point, a large wave lunged itself at the ship causing it to rock enough to throw some of the habitants of the bridge to the floor. Brody fell down like most of the others and then fought to push himself back onto his feet. "So, what do we do now?"

Everyone turned to the captain for an idea. The captain's motivation was for his ship and his crew. "We should turn back. If we head away from this area now, it might be our only chance to survive."

"I can't permit that," a dominating voice called out.

Everybody turned to perceive the source of the voice and they beheld Julianne standing in the doorway.

"With respect, miss, this is my ship and my crew," the captain asserted. "I have command here."

Julianne was no longer in the doorway, but up against the captain. "My authority supersedes that of any mortal," she declared before placing her right hand upon his forehead. The captain fell to the floor unconscious.

"What did you do to him?" Bridie asked insistently.

Within a second, Julianne was up against Bridie.

"No!" Brody cried out. "We are willing to cooperate. Don't hurt her."

"Your captain is only incapacitated," Julianne claimed. "I have no intention of permanently harming any of you, but we must continue to the island."

Mrs. LaGrance finally stepped forward. "The captain is only in charge of the ship," she told Julianne, "but I am the leader of this expedition. On my authority, we will endeavour to find your island."

Julianne was pleased with this exclamation. "What is your motivation, Mrs. LaGrance?"

"Money," Mrs. LaGrance revealed.

"You mean power."

"I mean influence."

Julianne moved herself to be standing before Mrs. LaGrance and she examined her closely. "You mean acceptance."

"I mean…" Mrs. LaGrance started, thinking she could come up with a better response. "Yes, I mean acceptance."

Julianne nodded. "Keep heading forward, ignore the dangers, and you will all find acceptance," she said. Julianne looked around at all the faces in the room. They were each looking nervously at her.

The captain coughed and flinched and then came to his senses. Julianne turned and strode magnificently out of the room.

"What happened?" the captain asked as he rose to his feet.

Before anybody could answer, another wave smashed against the side of the ship throwing them all to the deck. The impact of this wave seemed more substantial than previously and it caused a sudden ripple of urgency among the crew. The captain jumped to his feet and started yelling orders to everyone nearby. Every member of his crew followed his orders dutifully and immediately. Brody, Bridie, Zachary and Mrs. LaGrance stood by helplessly, relying on the expertise of the captain and his crew to navigate the storm.

"Non crew members please vacate the bridge," the captain insisted.

Brody took Bridie's hand and led her to the exit. Bridie wanted to object but she knew she didn't have any skills to help the crew, so she submitted to Brody's insistence that they both leave. Zachary and Mrs. LaGrance followed them. They all headed for the recreation lounge thinking mutually that the most useful thing they could all do was have something to drink.

"Is anybody else having second thoughts about this trip?" Zachary asked before taking a large gulp of brandy.

Brody and Bridie agreed. Mrs. LaGrance was too compelled by her greed to have any doubts. Brody handed Bridie a gin and tonic. She accepted the drink but had a look on her face.

"What?" Brody asked.

"You've got to stop doing boyfriend stuff," she said. "I should get my own drink. You didn't even ask what I wanted. That's such a couple thing."

Brody considered what she was saying. "You're right," he said, and he took her glass from her. "Can I get you a drink while I'm getting one?"

Bridie laughed. "Yes, alright. Thank you."

"What would you like?"

"A gin and tonic," Bridie said with irony.

Brody passed her back her original drink. She took a sip. "Now you're flirting with me," she accused.

"Oh god, I can't get anything right, can I?"

Bridie shook her head. "That's such a boyfriend thing to say."

Brody sighed and laughed. He took a sip from his bottle of Stella Artois. Everybody stood in silence for a moment and listened to the continuing crashing of the waves and commotion of the crew. They were all too nervous to sit down. Eventually, Bridie turned to Brody.

"Brody, if we're going to die today, this could be our last chance…" she said, taking hold of his hand.

Brody was ninety percent sure he knew what she was saying. "You mean… Netflix and chill?"

"Yes, I want you to Netflix and chill my brains out."

Brody smiled keenly at the idea, and he was quick to respond. "I'd love to, but I just don't think we should. We nearly ruined our friendship because of sex. We've come a long way on our journey together and we have to leave that chapter firmly in the past."

Bridie was surprised and impressed. "That's very noble, Brody, but this isn't a test. I really do want you to do me."

"Oh, thank god for that!" Brody exclaimed with libidinous relief, and he took hold of Bridie's arm to escort her out of the room.

After they had left, Zachary and Mrs. LaGrance were left alone in an awkward silence. Zachary peered at Mrs. LaGrance and wondered what she was thinking and if it was anything like what he was thinking. Zachary thought she wasn't a particularly attractive woman, but her dominating confidence gave her a certain allure.

"They're right, you know," Zachary eventually said. "This could be the end of the line for us all. We might as well go out with a bang as they say."

Mrs. LaGrance was shocked, but a little flattered. Men never ever propositioned her. "But you're married," she said.

"So are you," Zachary simply replied.

"Alright, you talked me into it," Mrs. LaGrance unexpectedly revealed and she grabbed his tie and led him, choking, out of the room.

About half an hour later, Brody and Bridie were slumped on the floor near to the bed in Bridie's cabin. They were both naked, panting and sweaty. Their sex had been brief but passionate. It had been brief because they didn't know how much time they had until whatever was going to happen happened. Bridie looked across at Brody and smiled.

"That was weird," she said.

"Yeah," Brody concurred. "It was like it was forbidden or something."

"Bad boy," she said coitally.

It was at this point that the ship seemed to explode. The two ex-lovers were thrown to opposite sides of the cabin as everything in the room scattered or dislodged. The room itself turned upside down and water started to gush in. Brody lifted his head up, using his hand to protect his face from enclosing debris and water. "Bridie!" he screamed. "Are you okay?"

"Not really," she replied, "but I'm alive."

Bridie's leg was hurting her a lot but it was under a load of stuff so she couldn't see what kind of state it was in. The gushing water became suddenly more, and Bridie found herself entirely underwater, out of the cabin and away from the ship. She thrashed around, ignoring the pain in her leg and she desperately tried to make out any visual sign of access to air. It seemed upwards would be a pretty good direction to go in, but she was so disoriented, she was having a hard time determining which way upwards was. After a few frantic moments she could see the ship, in the murky water, sinking away from her. This gave her the clue she needed to find up. She desperately propelled herself upwards towards what she could now just about make out to be the surface. The more energy she used to get herself to air, the more aware she became of how little longer she could survive without it. She didn't think she was going to make it. Her mind raced through everything important in her life – her work, her father, chocolate crepes for breakfast, her independence, wanting to have children one day, Brody…

Brody had been swept away from Bridie as the ship had submerged and he had found himself in a similar panic to Bridie's. Brody had barely had enough time to determine a plan of action before a plank of wood, which had been ripped from the deck of the ship, ploughed into Brody's head, knocking him unconscious.

## CHAPTER FOUR
## "SURVIVORS"

Zachary dragged his naked body out of the water and onto the beach. Mrs. LaGrance was pulling herself alongside him. She was also naked. The ship had wrecked while they were in the middle of their adulterous tryst. As his cabin had filled with water, Zachary had managed to get himself and Mrs. LaGrance outside and into the unforgiving, freezing cold water from where they had headed for shore.

Once Zachary was out of the water and on all fours on the warm beach, he let his body slump into the sand where he attempted to catch his breath. Mrs. LaGrance did the same. After his breathing settled enough for him to talk, he turned to look at his nude companion.

"Are you alright, Mrs. LaGrance?" he asked.

Mrs. LaGrance took a little while to reply, while she concentrated on her own breathing problems. "I think you can call me Karen, now," she said. "And, yes, I'm alright. Well, 'alright' is hardly the appropriate word. I'm more like some-right. I'm undamaged and breathing."

Zachary was feeling a little fitter now, so he turned to face the sun and he sat up. He decided the first thing they should do is look for other survivors. Scouring the lengthy beach, he could make out what looked like several bodies scattered around. The nearest one was as naked as they were.

"Come on!" he said.

Mrs. LaGrance wasn't ready to move yet. "Come on, where?"

"There's other people on the beach. I think we should see if anybody else is alive."

Mrs. LaGrance sat up quickly. "But I'm naked!" she shrieked trying to cover up all the parts she didn't want people to see.

"I don't think that's our first concern," Zachary chided her.

"You would if you had my body!"

Zachary wasn't sure what to say to this. "Fine, stay here if you want to, but I'm going to check out that naked girl over there."

"Oh, I see. That's why you're in such a rush!"

Zachary was already walking away from Mrs. LaGrance and towards the naked girl. "It's not because she's naked. It's because she's the nearest."

"Fine!" Mrs. LaGrance screamed at him, and she proceeded to sulk by turning onto her side, away from Zachary.

As he walked towards the girl, he turned and looked at Mrs. LaGrance's back. "Nice bum!" he teased her.

Mrs. LaGrance immediately covered up her bum with her left hand, and then flicked Zachary the finger. She looked around to see what she could cover herself up with. The beach was all around, leading up to a sheer cliff face. There was no greenery or vegetation nearby. There was only one option as far as she could tell. She would have to bury herself in the sand. Mrs. LaGrance turned onto her back and started shovelling sand onto her body until her intimate parts were covered. She then made herself a little sand pillow to elevate her head slightly, and then she turned her head and watched as Zachary reached the naked girl.

The girl was on her front. Zachary gently took hold of her arm and turned her over. Once she was on her back, Zachary could see it was Bridie. There didn't look to be any life in her. He felt for a pulse, but he'd never done it before, so he wasn't sure if he was doing it right. He couldn't feel anything in her wrist or in her neck. He thought he should probably administer cardiopulmonary resuscitation, but again, he'd never done it before. He had seen it done in the movies a hundred times, though, and he was pretty confident he could replicate the procedure. He began by pushing down rhythmically on Bridie's chest, being extremely careful not to touch her inappropriately. He then held her nostrils closed with a thumb and forefinger and attempted to breath his air into her mouth. After two attempts of this routine, Zachary was delighted and proud of himself as Bridie suddenly jerked to her left and started coughing water out of her lungs. Once she stopped wheezing, she then turned to look into the face of her saviour. She was a little surprised to see Zachary leaning over her without any clothes on.

"Why are you naked, Zachary?"

Zachary laughed. "You can talk."

Bridie's face fell a million miles and she looked down at herself. "Oh my god!" she screamed and attempted to cover herself with her hands in the same way Mrs. LaGrance had. "I'm completely naked."

Zachary stood up proudly without worrying about his nudity. "I'm surprised at you, Bridie. You are rebellious, and risk-taking, and forthright. I wouldn't have imagined being naked would bother you so much!"

Bridie looked at Zachary's body and admired his enormous self-confidence. She realised he was absolutely right and that she shouldn't be ashamed of her nakedness. Bridie moved her hands away from her breasts and her crotch and tried to look as confident as Zachary did about it. Zachary flashed her a smile. "Woof!"

"You dog!" Bridie cried at him with deliberate irony. "Don't look at me like that. You're old enough to be my father."

"I'm just messing with you. Shall we check on the others?"

"Others?" Bridie asked, suddenly realising that she had no idea where they were or what was going on. It's amazing how much being naked can distract you from other important issues. Bridie sat up and looked around the beach. She could see several bodies in various places. "Brody!" she cried, and then quickly got to her feet. "Brody!"

"Come on. Let's see if he's here," Zachary suggested as he walked towards the next nearest body.

Bridie jogged a few steps to catch up with him. "I drowned," she told him.

"What?"

They carried on walking. "The last thing I remember was swimming for the surface, but I wasn't anywhere near it when I passed out. I don't understand how I got to the beach."

"Well, just be happy that you did," Zachary suggested.

When they got to the next body, it was Edmund, Mrs. LaGrance's bodyguard. Edmund, of course, was fully clothed. They quickly revived him and then went to the next one.

"What about that one?" Bridie asked, pointing at Mrs. LaGrance.

"That's Karen… er, Mrs. LaGrance. She buried herself in the sand to cover up her nakedness."

"Why is she naked?" Bridie asked. "Come to think of it, why are you naked? I'm naked because me and Brody were naked when the ship got into trouble…"

As they headed towards the next of their unconscious companions, Zachary didn't answer Bridie's question. "Oh my god! You two were…"

"Shut up," he asked. "Just like you and Brody, we thought we were going to die,"

"Ew! But Mrs. LaGrance."

Zachary shrugged. "I like to be dominated. She likes to dominate."

"I don't want to know."

They arrived at the next body. This time it was one of the crew. They didn't know his name. He was already awake, but groggy. Near to him, Bridie could see Condy on her back a few feet away. Bridie ran over to her friend to see if she was breathing.

"Condy… Condy!" Bridie called to her. She gently slapped her face and shook her a little.

Condy suddenly came to life. "Get off. Get off me!" she cried out instinctively. Condy sat up suddenly and looked around at her surroundings. She then rested her eyes on Bridie.

"Bridie, you've got no clothes on."

"I know," Bridie replied sarcastically. "I feel like I'm having a nightmare. Next I'll have to do my A-levels again."

Condy smiled. She would have laughed in normal circumstances, but a smile was all she could manage for now.

"Are you okay?" Bridie asked her, watching her rubbing her arm.

"Yes, just a few bruises. How is everybody else?"

"No major injuries so far. Come on, we're still gathering people together."

By the time they'd checked all the bodies, they had found the captain and a handful of other crew members they didn't really know, but there was no Brody. Bridie had held back her emotions until now, but not finding Brody was too much for her and she fell down on her knees on the sand and wept. Zachary knelt down in front of her and put a comforting hand on her arm.

"I'm sorry," he said. "I was fond of Brody. He was a good man."

"He's not dead," Bridie said quietly without lifting her head.

"That's the spirit. At least the two of you sorted your shit out before… you know."

Bridie blubbed for a few more moments and then struggled hard to compose herself. "Yeah, I'm glad we did that."

The others that they had found on the beach were all shaken and in shock, but nobody was seriously hurt. They were gathering together nearby Bridie and Zachary. Condy was doing her best as a doctor to check for injuries and reassure the ones who were shaken the most. Altogether, there were nine survivors on the beach - Bridie, Zachary, Mrs. LaGrance, Condy, the captain, Edmund and three crew members.

"Does anybody have their phone with them?" Zachary had the sense to ask.

All the clothed members of the group searched their soaking clothes but only one member of the crew still had his phone, but it wouldn't switch on, presumably killed by the water. There was also a crack on the screen that hadn't been there before.

"Look!" one of the crew members cried out.

Everybody turned to look at the crew member. He was pointing out to the sea, so everybody then altered their view towards the sea. There was a woman coming out of the water, carrying a body. As they moved closer, some of them recognised that it was Julianne. She was calmly strolling from the water is if she was out for an afternoon amble. Bridie was anxious to see whose body it was she was carrying, although she soon became pretty sure it wasn't Brody because the body was wearing a crew uniform. Julianne fully emerged from the water and dropped the body onto the beach with very little care or ceremony.

"Hey, be careful!" Condy admonished.

"He's dead already," Julianne dismissed.

Condy ran over and checked the body Julianne had brought out of the water, to see if there were any life signs. His skin was pruned, his complexion was white, and Condy couldn't find a pulse. Despite the fact that he was clearly dead, Condy tried to resuscitate him for about a minute. It didn't do any good.

"What happened to my ship?" asked the captain.

"It sank," Julianne replied.

"And it's your fault," the captain emotionally claimed.

"Yes, it is," Julianne replied without fear or remorse. "No vessels are permitted on the island. The only way for me to get here was to get as close as possible before the island's natural defences smashed your ship into bits."

"And you let most of my crew die!" the captain growled.

"And I saved the rest of you!" Julianne told them. "But I didn't have time to get the rest before they gave up on life."

"Gave up on life?" Condy cried.

"You mortals are so fragile. It's amazing there are so many of you. I tried to save the important ones first and then I got as many of the others as I could."

"Brody was important," Bridie said to her, tearfully. "Why didn't you save him?"

"Which one was Brody?"

"My boyfriend… ex-boyfriend. My best friend."

Julianne nodded. "Oh, yes. I looked for him, but he wasn't there."

"He wasn't there?"

"Yes. He must have drowned more quickly than the others."

Bridie bit her bottom lip attempting to keep back the tears. "Do you think you could go back and find his body?"

"There isn't time," Julianne replied resolutely. "I am going to the centre of the island. I suggest you all come with me, for safety."

Everybody watched, speechless, as Julianne turned to her left and strode down the beach. They all looked at each other, waiting for someone to make a decision.

"You heard her!" said a voice behind them. "Let's go."

Everyone else turned around and saw that it was the naked Mrs. LaGrance who had spoken. She had emerged from her shallow, self-employed sandy grave and was now standing before them with everything hanging out. One of the crew members spontaneously started taking his clothes off.

"What are you doing?" another crewman asked him.

The undressing crewman shrugged. "When in Rome…"

Mrs. LaGrance cast aside her doubts about her nakedness and she waltzed confidently in Julianne's wake. Zachary quickly followed, and slowly, so did all the others.

Condy decided to walk with Bridie.

"Why aren't you bothered about being completely naked?"

"Well, it's kind of apt, I think, if this turns out to be Eden." Bridie said and she continued to tell Condy about her final tryst with Brody and the reason why Zachary and Mrs. LaGrance were naked.

"But they're both married!" Condy exclaimed prudishly.

"Unhappily," Bridie said as a potential excuse.

As the travelling party followed the curve of the beach they found themselves entering a boding, yet beautiful forest. Julianne strode into the forest fearlessly, but the others were trepidatious to say the least, and the naked ones were concerned about pricks, thorns and nettles.

"How far is it to the centre of the island?" Zachary asked Julianne as the sun and relative safety of the beach disappeared behind them.

"In your terms, it is approximately one day of travel."

"A day!" Condy exclaimed. "Then we should gather provisions."

Several people nodded in agreement.

"Provisions?" Julianne asked. "Oh, yes. I keep forgetting you are mortals and require sustenance."

Julianne stopped walking and turned to face the shipwrecked company. "I will allow one hour for the gathering of provisions, and then we must resume the journey."

Everybody looked at somebody else. The captain put his hand in the air, somewhat ironically.

"Excuse me, but what provisions do you suggest we gather?"

Julianne was confused, and a little annoyed by this question. "It was your insistence that you gather provisions. I don't see how it is my place to decree which provisions you gather."

Zachary decided to attempt to clarify. "I think what he's trying to say is that, although it is extremely supportive of you to give us time for the gathering of provisions, we have no idea what provisions there are to gather."

Julianne's understanding wasn't any better. "Do you people eat… fruit?" she asked.

The whole crowd nodded and answered to the affirmative.

"Then gather fruit!"

"The problem is," one of the crew who had worked in the ship's galley began. He walked over to a tree and pulled an odd-looking purple fruit from its branches. "We haven't seen fruit like this before. We don't know if it's healthy or poisonous."

"Ah!" Julianne exclaimed. "None of the fruit on this island will bring you harm. The reason you don't recognise the fruit in this forest is that it has been designed specifically for the appetites and needs of the simple-minded wild animals that dwell here, so it should be perfectly adequate for your needs."

"Charming," Mrs. LaGrance groaned.

Many of the crew were beginning to take umbrage at Julianne's attitude, but were all too intimidated to say anything about it. As a group they began taking berries from bushes, and some of them even climbed a few trees to release some of the bigger, juicier looking offerings of the forest. The crewman who used to work in the ship's galley, decided to brave an approach to Julianne.

"Miss Julianne? Erm, fruit is all very well, but ideally we need variety in order to sustain us. Essentially, we need meat, protein."

"Of course," Julianne replied kindly. "There is a source of meat which is easily attainable."

"Brilliant!" the crewman said, pleased with himself for making some progress with Julianne.

"What is your name?" she asked him.

"Dave," he said.

"Dave," Julianne addressed him respectfully, "Which one of your party would you like me to kill?"

Dave didn't understand the reason for her question straight away, but it soon struck him. "Oh, no, no. We aren't cannibals, Julianne. We don't kill each other for food."

"Then, what *do* you kill each other for?"

Dave laughed, thinking it was a much more intelligent question than it seemed. In fact, it wasn't a question at all, but a statement. "Sport, politics, religion," Dave suggested as three of the innumerable reasons man kills man.

"It won't be necessary to kill anybody," Julianne said. "There are other sources of meat for your digestion."

"Thank god for that."

"Indeed you should. The main source of the meat I refer to are the bodies of your erstwhile crewman bobbing about in the water, and that man I left on the beach."

"Oh," Dave sighed. "That's not going to go down very well."

"We aren't rugby players who have plane-crashed on the Andes," Bridie quipped. Nobody laughed, nor did they even understand the reference. "Nobody's seen that film? Alive? Sorry, that's Brody's influence. He and I watched a lot of films together."

"The point is," Dave said, trying to get the conversation back on track, "that we don't eat our own species."

Julianne considered this information. "But you eat other species?"

"Yes, that's right."

"You eat all other species?"

Dave raised his eyebrows and nodded. "Pretty much, yes."

"That's not really fair to the other species', is it?"

Dave hesitated, and so did everyone else listening to the conversation. "Well, we feel..."

"I mean, humans are the dominating species on the planet," Julianne interrupted, "and how are you taking care of your neighbours? You eat them! You eat the minorities, and you keep your butcher's knives away from the majority. And you dare to call this morality! You people are twisted," Julianne blasted them.

"Some of us are vegetarian," another member of the crew volunteered.

"Ah, yes, vegetarians. That's completely the wrong idea. Nothing ever grows or evolves if you are exclusive. You have to be inclusive if you are to learn, and that means eating both animal and human flesh. If you refuse any food group, all you are doing is limiting your growth."

Everybody paused to consider Julianne's philosophy. The scientists in the group all thought the idea had logical merit, but it lacked sociological or moral perspective. Some other members of the group were deciding who they would like to eat first.

"Let's just say," Dave said to Julianne, "that we're just not ready to take that step yet."

"Well, evolution takes a long time," Julianne replied facetiously. She then waved Dave away dismissively. "Do your part. Collect fruit with your friends."

Dave joined the group and for a while they all picked berries and climbed or shook trees to gather fruit. Everybody ate their fill as they collected, but slowly they all began to realise the same problem.

"How are we going to carry all this fruit?"

Julianne was the only one to offer a solution. "Take off your clothes and make them into bags."

This suggestion was met with a frankly embarrassed pause. "What?" Condy said.

"Half of you are naked already. It's a logical solution."

Everybody who was wearing clothes, froze in the fear that she was serious and that they might be obliged to comply. The naked ones were all standing proudly, looking expectantly at the others. Edmund looked encouragingly at Condy. Condy returned his gaze, knowing exactly what he was thinking.

"I will if you will," he said to her.

Condy laughed. She was laughing for two reasons. The first was because of her escalating realisation that Edmund had a thing for her. The second was out of nervousness for the inevitability of what was going to happen next. She looked pleadingly at her friend, Bridie, but Bridie was on the naked side of the argument, being already sans-clothing. Condy gave a loud sigh, placed the fruit she was carrying on the ground, and proceeded to unbutton her top. Edmund grinned like a giddy child and unzipped his trousers. Soon after this, everybody was naked. They started tying knots in the sleeves and trousers of their clothing so that they could fill them up with fruit and berries.

"Time to go!" Julianne bellowed at the group, and she headed further into the forest. Julianne's followers gathered their fruit 'bags' and continued on their journey. Condy couldn't believe how often she found herself glancing at Edmund. She had never found him attractive before now, but this was the first time she'd noticed how tight his body was. It made sense. He was a personal bodyguard and probably worked out a lot. Condy was especially surprised at herself because that wasn't what she looked for in a man. Intellectual compatibility had always been her number one factor, but she couldn't deny those abs… or that behind. Edmund turned suddenly and saw her looking at him. Condy immediately looked away, feeling foolish, ashamed and busted. As the exodus pushed deeper into the forest, the sun became lower in the sky. After a few hours of travel, the sky became distinctly twilight and many members of the group were exhausted.

"We should stop!" the captain suggested eventually. Many members of the group voiced their acquiescence.

"No," Julianne asserted. "We must continue. There is no reason to stop."

"Perhaps not for you," Condy said. "But we mortals are exhausted. We don't have unlimited energy like you appear to have. Plus, we are all naked and getting cold now that the sun is low. We should make camp and build a fire before nightfall."

Julianne finally stopped walking, realising she had no choice but to attend to the needs of the mortals. She turned and looked at the group. Nobody could quite understand how but it felt like Julianne was looking each of them in the eye simultaneously. "Very well. Make your camp. But we resume our journey the moment the sunlight returns to the sky."

Everybody breathed a sigh of relief, dropped the clothes containing the supplies and they sank to the ground to rest their legs and backs. They all had a little something to eat and engaged in light chatter while constantly trying desperately to ignore each other's nakedness.

"Does anybody know how to start a fire?" the captain asked. Most people were surprised that he didn't know how to do it himself.

"Rub two sticks together!" Zachary replied with a hint of ridicule.

The captain sighed. "Go on, then."

Zachary submitted to the captain's point. "Alright, it's a little more complicated than that, but it can't be too hard."

"Julianne?" Condy said to the immortal.

Julianne had been listening to their conversation with some amusement, although it never showed on her face. "Yes, Condy?"

"Do you know how to make fire?"

Julianne simply picked up two small sticks from the ground, struck them together once, and a fireball emerged, settling itself on the ground in the midst of the group. The fireball seemed to be perpetually burning with nothing to fuel it. Everybody stared in awesome amazement.

"Thanks," Condy said.

"Y'welcome."

The naked humans all gathered around the miraculous campfire, talking for a while and yawning with increasing frequency. Eventually one of the crew, whose name, it turned out, was Nigel, fell asleep. Julianne watched Nigel for about a minute before interrupting the conversation.

"Is he alright?" she asked, pointing at Nigel.

Some members of the group thought her question was funny.

"He's just asleep," Condy said.

"Asleep?" Julianne replied with curiosity. When Julianne had stolen the English language from Bridie on their first encounter, there were many concepts she had learned but not had the opportunity to address yet. Sleep was one of them. "I see. Sleep. Why do you do that?"

Nobody quite knew what to say to this.

"To be honest, we don't really know what sleep is for," Condy said eventually. "We used to think it was a way of storing or conserving energy, but we don't believe that anymore."

"Don't we?" the captain asked with surprise.

"Studies have shown that the amount of energy we conserve by sleeping is practically zero. It simply is not efficient."

"Then, don't do it," Julianne suggested.

"We don't have a choice. Sleep happens eventually whether we want it to or not. It's like urinating. Eventually, you've got to go."

"Urinating?" Julianne asked. "Oh, the excretion of waste liquids."

"Anyway. Scientists now think sleep is a kind of reboot switch. While we're awake, our minds fill up with all sorts of information, and we need download time for our brains to file it. And that probably accounts for dreams."

"Dreams?" Julianne asked.

Condy just laughed. "Never mind, Julianne. Count yourself blessed that you don't have to worry about any of these things."

"I am curious, though," she said. "Maybe I could try sleep. How do you do it?"

All the naked mortals looked at each other, in detail. "Well, I suppose, you just lie down, close your eyes and wait to fall asleep."

Julianne followed Condy's instructions as closely as possible. She laid on her back and closed her eyes. Everybody watched her silently as she lay there completely still. Nothing happened for about a minute. "So, how do I know when I'm asleep?"

"Erm," Condy thought about it. "Well, you don't. That's sort of the point. Being asleep is about losing your consciousness. It's like letting your mind descend into a void of no sensation of any kind."

Julianne sat up and opened her eyes. “I see. It sounds similar to my hibernation.”

“Yes, of course!” Condy exclaimed, remembering how Julianne had been when they found her. “Like your hibernation, except that sleep typically lasts between four and eight hours at a time, and we do it once a day.”

Julianne frowned. “That’s an extremely time-consuming activity for creatures who have a limited lifespan.”

Condy sniggered at this. She was joined by a number of the crew. “Yes, it is.”

“But as you obviously deem it necessary, I will leave you to sleep,” Julianne said, and she left the group walking just out of sight. “I will return with the sun.”

After that, there was a little more conversation and one by one they all fell asleep for the night.

Julianne sat at the edge of their camp, silently watching over them, waiting patiently for the morning to arrive.

## CHAPTER FIVE
## "SURVIVOR"

His dreams were about water. He was drowning, but he wasn't drowning. He was panicking about being under the water but, somehow, he was breathing. And he was hungry, starving. He had fruit on his mind – apples, bananas, pears, but especially strawberries. He had a vicious craving for strawberries. A school of strawberries swam by too far away for him to catch. He believed he was dreaming, but he was also afraid that he wasn't. This had to be a dream, but what if it was reality? What if he really was drowning, and this fantasy was his mind making him think it was a dream to make his drowning easier to deal with?

Brody woke up. It seemed obvious now – of course he had been dreaming. A school of strawberries? How could he have doubted it was a dream? His eyes were open, but he couldn't see anything. He strained as much as he could to make out any images at all, but after a while, all he could see were shadows. He heard his stomach rumble. He really was starving. That must have been why he was dreaming of fruit. He realised he could smell strawberries. Maybe he was in a field of strawberries? And maybe it was night? That would explain the darkness. His eyes were slowly beginning to adjust, and he could now make out the distant stars in the sky. He was lying on something soft. Maybe strawberries. Or maybe it was just mud, although it felt sandy.

Something stooped over him and blocked out the stars. Brody didn't know whether to panic or stay still. The smell of strawberries was overwhelming now. He felt a brush of hair fall briefly on his face and then it drifted away. He realised that someone, probably a woman or a long-haired man, was looking down on him. It was too dark to make out facial features or even the shape of a head, but by the way she moved, Brody was certain she was female. Something about her movement demonstrated that she was a young woman.

He felt a soft hand on his forehead. The hand was gentle, caressing, nurturing. It made him think of Bridie, which in turn created a lot of questions in his head. He slowly sat up. The young woman sat back to accommodate his movements.

"Where am I?" he asked.

The woman said nothing, but she stopped moving as if something had startled or distressed her.

"Do you understand me?" he asked her. Her shape was a little more discernible from his new perspective, but only a little.

The woman stood up, leaving Brody sitting up on the soft ground, and he watched her walk away.

"Where are you going?" he asked her desperately. "Did you rescue me from the water?"

The young woman walked out of sight. Brody kept his eyes fixed on that area. A few moments later, he saw a flame emerging from where the woman had gone. The flame moved closer to him and as it emerged, he realised the young woman was carrying a primitive torch, a flaming stick. As she came closer, Brody could make her out much more clearly. The first thing he noticed was that she was naked. She was naked and beautiful. He could make out the features of her face now, and she was devastatingly cute. Her brown hair was messy and dirty, but it was also frizzy and alluring. When she reached Brody, she stood before him for a few moments and he studied her gorgeous naked form in detail. He also realised that when she had walked away just now, she had taken the smell of strawberries with her, and now it had returned. The young woman knelt down beside him and planted the torch in the sand next to them. She peered into his eyes and she looked heavenly. Her facial expression wasn't telling Brody anything about what she was thinking, but she seemed to be kindly and curious.

"Who are you?" he eventually asked.

The woman simply shook her head slightly and then put her fingertips on his lips as if to inform him that talking is forbidden. Brody gently took hold of the woman's wrist and moved her hand away from his lips.

"Can you talk?" he asked.

The woman put her hand on his lips again, but a little more firmly this time.

"Is talking not allowed?" he asked, realising it was a pretty stupid question.

The woman pressed her fingers a little harder onto his lips. Brody, as tenderly as he could, took hold of her wrist once again and manoeuvred her hand from his lips to her own. She didn't resist, nor did she seem to fear him at all.

"Talk?" he asked, simply.

The young woman moved her fingers from her lips and opened her mouth as if she was lightly gagging. She did this a number of times and then pointed inside her mouth with her forefinger. Brody got the message. She was telling him that she wasn't capable of speech.

"So, you don't understand me?" he said to her, realising, once again, what a stupid question he had asked. "So, if I tell you that you are the most beautiful thing I have ever seen in my life, you won't get creeped out?"

The young woman smiled and, for a moment, Brody almost thought she understood, but it seemed it was just a smile. She put her hand on his brow as if she was feeling his temperature. He didn't object. It was a very pleasant sensation. Her eyes were nervous. She was looking all around him, at his forehead, at her own hand, at his chest, at his lips, at his…

Brody suddenly realised he was naked!

And every time she looked fleetingly at his eyes, she smiled again. It was a homely, teasing, familiar smile that made his heart swell. The caress of her fingertips on his face was overwhelmingly sensual, and he began to imagine that something undeniably erotic was happening between them. Was she just being friendly, or was she drawn to him in the way that he was to her? She put her other hand on his face and stroked his cheek. Brody was getting very strong positive signals from the feral girl, and the building sexual tension hovering between them created a physical manifestation in Brody's body.

The feral girl glanced down and saw Brody's body's offering to her, and instead of retreating from the situation, she looked into his eyes, her face beaming with possibility, but she did take her hands away from him. Her eyes were confident now, and she continued to stare at Brody with a kind of gentle lust, despite the fact that she was clearly giving Brody a signal to calm down a little. Brody was happy to comply with whatever the girl wanted from him. Yes, he was horny for her, but the thought of having sex with a beautiful feral girl he had met only minutes ago seemed a little too perverted, even for him. Who was he kidding? It was a dream come true. They gazed at each other for several moments. Brody's physical excitement slowly started to behave itself. As he watched her, he wished so much that they could communicate.

Brody put the palm of his hand on his chest. "Brody," he told her.

The feral girl didn't seem to understand.

He patted himself on the chest as if to hammer home the point. "Brody," he repeated. "My name is Brody."

The girl watched him in confusion for a couple of seconds and then she took his hand from his chest and placed it on her own. Brody's hand was now, at her insistence, firmly pressed against her naked chest and his physical manifestation of lust returned. He withdrew his hand from her chest and, instead, interlocked his fingers with hers so that they could hold hands. He wanted to know if she had a name, but he was aware that asking her wouldn't be fruitful. She leaned forwards and spontaneously kissed him on the nose. It was such a surprising move, that Brody giggled. She continued to smile at him as she pulled back from the kiss. The smell of strawberries emanating from her was overwhelming.

"Strawberry," he suggested. "No, I can't call you strawberry. But maybe something related to strawberries."

As Brody talked to himself, the girl watched him, enchanted.

"I once had a colleague who was a botanist and he would talk all the time about the Latin names for, and etymological roots of plants and flowers. I have a very good memory, and Gary would repeat the same things all the time, so if I remember correctly, the strawberry belongs to the genus Fragaria, which is of the rose family…" Brody's auto-conversation tailed off at this thought and he stared at the girl's gorgeous, smiling face. "Rose," he said.

The girl flinched slightly, almost as if she recognised the word.

"I'm going to call you Rose," Brody continued. "Is that okay?"

Rose paused and then slightly nodded as if to agree. Brody realised it was probably just a random movement of her head and not an expression of agreement, but he took it as acceptance that, from now on, she would be called Rose.

"Rose," he said, pointing his finger gently at her chest. "Rose," he repeated.

Rose took hold of his hand and nodded again. Brody began to wonder if she could understand him, to some extent. They seemed to be communicating.

There was no doubt there existed some kind of chemistry between them.

Rose sat back slightly, and then she timidly pointed her finger at her own chest while keeping her eyes fixed on Brody's. She then put her two hands together by joining her fingers and thumbs, and she formed a shape that looked to Brody like a heart. She held the shape there for a few moments, and Brody watched in astonishment. Rose, for the final part of her statement to Brody, pointed her finger at his chest, and then she laid her hands to rest near her feet as she sat before him, with her legs crossed.

Brody was boggled by what he'd seen. The three-part message she was conveying couldn't be any clearer. "You love me?" he translated, dubiously. Rose had pointed to herself, made a heart shape and then pointed at him. What else could she have meant?

Rose watched Brody expectantly as if she was waiting for him to reflect the sentiment. In his heart, Brody wanted to say it. He had an overwhelming compulsion to tell her he loved her too, but his brain was too prevalent to let him just blurt it out. He also realised he was somewhat traumatised after not only the events on the boat but also finding himself wherever he currently was, in the dark, being nursed by the cutest naked girl he had ever been nursed by, so he was nowhere near level-headed enough to understand what he was thinking or feeling.

After a few moments of Rose watching Brody think these thoughts, she turned and crawled out of the light. Not wanting to let her go, Brody grabbed her foot just before it went out of reach. He heard

Rose giggle. It was adorable. It was also telling that she had a voice. Her giggle told him she had vocal cords and that maybe she just didn't have a language. Rose didn't take her foot any further away from him, but she seemed to be stretching to reach something. Once she had reached the thing, whatever it was, she twisted herself back round to sit in front of Brody again. When Brody saw what she had in her hand, he laughed, and felt kind of silly. In her hand was an apple. It was clear to Brody now, that the hand gesture hadn't meant to be a heart, it had meant to be an apple. She was offering to give him an apple, not telling him that she loved him. Brody took the apple, and he smiled at her appreciatively. He was starving.

"Thank you," he said, knowing that the words wouldn't mean anything to her. He thought about what he could do to express his thanks. He leaned over and kissed Rose on the nose in the same way she had done to him earlier. Rose bit her lip coquettishly and giggled again.

Brody took a large bite of the apple. It was delicious. He fancied it was the most scrumptious apple he had ever set his taste-buds upon. This sensation was probably just because he was starving and lost and slightly infatuated with his Rose, so everything seemed other-worldly and magical. After he had eaten the apple, she fetched him a variety of other foods, mainly fruit, some of which he couldn't recognise. There was even some white meat which could have been chicken. The food was presented to him on a crude plate made from some kind of rock or slate. It was occurring to Brody that, wherever he was, Rose's culture hadn't been touched by modern civilisation. He had giving some of his time since waking to considering where he was. It was possible he was on the island that Julianne had told them about, that Condy had suggested might be Eden. Or it could just be some undiscovered, ordinary island.

Once Brody had finished his repast, he handed the plate appreciatively to Rose. Rose had joined him and eaten a little food as well. She placed the plates on the ground and then turned to look at Brody. Brody so wished she could talk to him. He had so many questions. The first of which would have been along the lines of "Will you go out for a drink with me?"

Rose edged close to him and she put her hands tenderly on his arms. Brody relaxed and decided to let her do whatever she wanted to do to him. Rose affectionately slid her hands up Brody's arms until they were at his shoulders. Then, she softly pushed him backwards as a signal for him to lie down. Brody laid on his back and watched her eyes as she shuffled herself up against him until their naked thighs were not just touching but pressed against each other. Brody was both apprehensive and excited about what she might do next. She leaned down slowly, kissed him on the nose again, and then laid down next to him, laying her head on his chest and draping her arm across his belly. Brody realised that she was expecting him to get some sleep, despite the fact that he'd just woken up. However, it was the middle of the night, so he didn't object to her wishes. He didn't know if he could sleep, but he was perfectly happy to lie there, watching the stars until the morning with Rose's warm body cuddled up with him. It was a wonderful, comforting sensation and an unbelievably erotic and sensational experience.

Brody didn't sleep at all. He was far too anxious about his predicament. He was desperate to find out where he was and, more importantly, if anybody else from his party had survived. Rose appeared to be asleep already. Brody considered gently rolling her off his chest and going for an exploration, but he didn't have the heart or the will to leave her, even if it was just for a short while. She seemed so fond of him that he couldn't help but share her compassion. He was feeling extraordinarily protective towards her. From the little interaction they had shared, Brody could see in her eyes that she was kind and gentle, but also there was strength behind her gaze. The kind of strength you would need to survive in the wild. He wondered for the first time if she was alone. He had assumed there were others but as far as he knew, she could be the only one there. Suddenly it made sense. Of course she was attached to him if he was the only company she had. He realised he had wrapped his arms around her while he had been lost in thought. He made a decision to be with her from now on, to stay with her or to take her with him wherever he went. If she wanted to, of course.

Rose was snoring. Nothing earth-shattering, just a gentle, rhythmic purring that was so adorable he almost wished she would never wake up. Brody lay there for hours, listening to Rose's purr and watching the horizon as the sun slowly came up over the far away hills. As the sun arrived, it was the first time Brody got a good look at his surroundings. The ground that they were lying on was a kind of sand-mud mixture covering a huge beach. They were quite a way inland, but he could see the ocean not too far away to his left. To Brody's right were acres of pastures and trees and great varieties of plants and flowers with a seemingly endless range of mountains in the background. Brody took in the breath-taking scenery but nothing had pleased his aesthetic taste quite like the girl who was asleep upon him.

It was maybe an hour after dawn that Rose awoke. Brody could feel her head rubbing slowly up and down his chest as she came to consciousness. Her long brown hair tickled his ribs as she turned her head to face him. Brody brushed hair away from her face to reveal a gorgeous sleepy morning smile.

Brody couldn't help but smile in return. "Morning," he said. She returned his greeting with another kiss on the nose. Brody wondered why she was always kissing him on the nose, not that he minded. It was a delightful little trait. Maybe she wasn't alone here after all and nose-kissing was a custom of her people.

Rose lifted herself from Brody's body and sat before him. She simply stroked his arm affectionately for a few moments, and then she stood up and walked a few feet away to a strange cart constructed from wood and tied together with vines. Inside the cart, Rose took some more of the food she had fed him in the night. Brody wondered if she had made the cart herself or if it belonged to her people. While Brody had been lying awake in the night, he had eventually come to the conclusion that it made very little sense to suppose she was on the island completely alone and that there must be more people like her around somewhere. They ate their fruity breakfast with a little bit of meat and had conversation with their eyes and body language. Brody couldn't quite get over what seemed to be happening between him and this mute island girl. It was like a bizarre fantasy or one of those tantalising dreams where you meet the perfect girl and then you wake up and realise you just made her up. He tried to shake off the idea that he was dreaming because it was too devastating to contemplate. He looked Rose in the eye and found himself staring at her so that he could remember every feature of her face in case he woke up. But this couldn't possibly be a dream. It felt too real. It was tangible. Brody touched Rose's face, gently caressing her right cheek and absorbing the sensation for any signs of fallacy or insubstantiality. He felt nothing virtual, Rose was so real. She lifted her hand and mirrored Brody's actions. They sat there for a long time, just touching each other's faces. Brody entertained the overly sentimental, ridiculously melodromantic thought that he would be happy to stay here alone with Rose for the rest of his life. During their caressing session, Rose kept smiling and then blushing and occasionally biting her bottom lip. After a couple of minutes, Brody was overcome with passion and amour, and so he decided he had to kiss her, properly. He leaned in and charged his pursed lips towards hers, keeping eye contact with her in order to determine whether his kiss was welcome. To his surprise, despite the obvious chemistry between them, Rose pulled away as Brody approached her lips. Noticing this hesitation, Brody halted his advance and began, slowly, to pull back. Rose shook her head but put her hand on Brody's cheek. She leaned in and kissed him on the nose again. Rose moved her hand from his cheek and put a single finger on his lips. Brody understood this to mean that she didn't want to kiss him on the lips. The last thing he wanted was to create a misunderstanding or to upset Rose, so he nodded his head.

"I'm sorry," Brody said to her and he believed she understood. Rose smiled at first, and then she looked upset. Her eyes dropped down and she turned her head as if she was contemplating something. Brody interpreted this new behaviour as conflict. Rose seemed to be battling some confused feelings. She stood up and turned away from him and then turned back and looked him in the face. Her breathing had visibly increased. Brody watched her naked chest heaving more excessively. Rose put her hands on her hips and swayed slightly. She was clearly worried about something. She knelt down in front of him again and rocked gently, gazing at his eyes. She leaned forwards and put her forehead on his. Brody wished he knew what was upsetting her. He felt helpless. He hated seeing her like this and not being able to comfort or protect her. She kissed him on the nose again and then thrust her hand through his hair and planted her moist lips on his mouth, pressing hard with passion. Brody more-than-willingly reciprocated her kiss and they completed their aural embrace by mating their tongues. Rose continued to press her face and then her body against Brody with a passion that bordered on aggression, even fury, and she pushed him right down onto his back, still kissing, and mounted him. Both Brody and Rose fought to breathe through their noses as they were unwilling to disconnect. Rose manoeuvred her abdomen over his lower body so that she could tease his desire and it didn't take long before they were having sex. If Brody had had any time to think it through, he might have been gallant and restrained but she wasn't really giving him any choice. The sex was furious and intense. Rose was an animal, a spirit of unrestrained grinding passion which caused the act to be brief but satisfying. They were in perfect union and managed to finish at roughly the same time. And once it was over, Rose wouldn't let Brody just lie there panting and catching his breath. She jumped to her feet and started to dance. It was a strange, unique, erotic and extemporaneous dance which had a beautiful, perfect, almost mathematic rhythm. Rose's eyes were closed and she moved like a professional. Dancing without music is risky and can look silly, but Rose pulled it off big time. After a minute or so, she opened her eyes again, pulled Brody to his feet and indicated that she wanted him to dance with her. Brody wasn't a dancer. In fact, he hated it. He didn't consider himself capable. Rose could sense this and so she took his hands and directed him. Slowly at first, she built a rhythm by swaying him from side to side, looking into his eyes, begging him to trust her. He did. She took his hands and made patterns in the air with him, and she smiled broadly at his cooperation. As their jive intensified, Brody let go of all his inhibitions and relaxed himself into Rose's hands, letting her lead him in their movement for what seemed like a blissful eternity. At its peak, their passion dance erupted into a flurry of wild gestures which, to Brody's amazement, were compatible and reliant on each other. Rose and Brody danced as if they were following the same instinctive choreography without missing a beat or dropping a move. And after the climax, they concluded by holding each other and swaying while slowly turning in the manner of newlyweds doing their first dance on their wedding night. With their faces buried in each other's shoulders, Rose and Brody were the only people in the universe, both discovering something more essential than anything they had felt before.

About half an hour later, Brody was lying on the warm sand in the sun with Rose draped across his chest just like the night before, both drenched in the sweat of their lovemaking and dancing. Exhausted, Brody quickly fell asleep under a hypnotic sensation of contentment. He would have almost considered that being free from the traps of civilisation and laying with a girl whose only flaw was that she couldn't speak, he had everything he needed. The only thing that ruined his rejoicing was that he missed his friends, especially Bridie. Brody finally drifted to sleep dreaming images of Bridie and Rose fighting over him in a mud pit. Rose won the fight, but they were all friends afterwards. Next, Brody was dreaming he was drowning again. The harder he swam towards the surface, the further away he was from it. Eventually he gave up but before Brody drowned, Iain, the ship's psychiatrist, popped up in front of him.

"Hello, Bu… Bu… Brody," Iain said.

Brody was a bit stuck for what to say. "Erm… I'm a bit busy at the moment, Iain."

"Drowning?"

"Trying not to."

Iain put a comforting hand on Brody's struggling shoulder. "Everything will be alright. I will find you, and then we can go home."

Brody paused while simultaneously fighting with the water. "I'm not sure I want to go home."

"Because of her?" Iain asked, his voice harbouring a hint of approval.

Brody was surprised for a moment until he remembered that he was dreaming and that Iain was borne from his own subconscious. "Partly. Also, we came here to explore. If the others didn't make it, I owe it to them as well as myself to finish what we came here for."

"Rubbish!" Ian exclaimed. "It's because of the girl. You don't want to leave her. You've known her less than a day."

"I know, but she has enchanted me," he said with unashamed drama. "If we leave, I'm bringing her with me."

Iain paused. "There is still hope," he replied ambiguously.

When Brody awoke from his dream, the sun was still hot in the sky. As his consciousness returned, Brody quickly realised that Rose wasn't resting on him anymore. He sat up sharply and three-sixtied the beach in search of her. She wasn't anywhere to be seen. Brody panicked. It was a double panic. He panicked because he was worried that he'd lost her, and he also panicked because the thought of losing her hurt so much. What had this girl done to him to make him so dependant of her so quickly? He got up onto his knees and scoured the beach again, as if the extra few inches of height would give him a radically greater perspective. Strangely enough, it seemed to work, as he noticed movement in the water a few feet from the shore. He stood up and slightly staggered towards it, and the movement he'd seen slowly turned into the shape of Rose emerging from the water. Before he could stop himself or act cool about it, he was running towards her, ecstatic that she was there. When he caught up to her, he threw himself at her, clasping his arms around her shoulders and flinging the two of them into the water. When their heads bobbed up out of the ocean, Brody saw such delight on Rose's face for his reaction, that he almost wept. He brushed her soaking brown hair away from her face so that he could see her gorgeous smile. He felt her hands on his back under the water and she pulled herself closer to him. They kissed, and then they stepped out of the water, onto the shore.

"Hey, Rose," he said to her through a smile that simply wouldn't diminish.

Rose stood on the tips of her toes and leaned in to kiss Brody on the nose. Rose took hold of Brody's hand and she led him back to shore. They walked to where Rose had left her crudely built cart, and then Rose used gestures to compel Brody to sit. He did as he was told. Rose knelt in front of the cart and started rummaging through it.

"I had a dream," Brody started to tell her. "It was about a friend of mine. Well, not really a friend.

More of a father figure, in a way. He was always giving me advice and often pushing me in the right direction. Well, not even necessarily the right direction, but he had a way of making sure I chose a direction."

Rose listened to Brody's voice. She couldn't understand anything he was saying, but she liked the sound. It was soothing and commanding at the same time. Rose found what she was looking for in the cart. It was a large, old folded up sheet of paper. She opened it up and laid it on the ground in front of them both. It was a map of the island. Brody carried on talking.

"Anyway, in the dream he told me that he was looking for me and he said that when he found me, he would take me back home."

Rose pointed at the map on the edge of the paper facsimile of the island. Brody examined it and then Rose swept her arm around in a semi-circle as if to demonstrate their surroundings. She was telling him that 'you are here' on the map. Brody nodded to express that he understood.

"The thing is, I want to see Iain again," Brody continued, "I want to see my friends. I have one special friend, my best friend, that I hope I haven't lost. And I hope you and she will get along."

Rose then pointed at an area on the map that was quite deep within the island, but still on the eastern edge. Brody examined it. It looked like the distance between the two places was quite a walk but, without scale, he couldn't really determine it for certain.

"And I do want to go home, and I want to get back to my work, but there's a serious problem. I think I've fallen in love with you," he said nervously, watching Rose to see if she gave any reaction, which she didn't. "And I can only go home if you'll come with me. And if you won't, or you can't come with me, then, what I'm saying is…"

Rose covered the line from where they were to where they were going on the map with her two fingers representing legs walking the distance. She then looked up at Brody expectantly.

Brody looked into her eyes and finished his sentence. "… what I'm saying is I'll follow you anywhere."

Rose continued to look at him. She hadn't understood anything Brody had said, and she was waiting for some confirmation. Brody kissed her on the nose again. She seemed to take this as a yes. Brody realised that the kiss on the nose seemed to be a kind of universal positive, a way of expressing general warm, good feelings and assuring thoughts. Rose smiled, happily at his reply and then she kissed him on the mouth. They stayed that way for a while before preparing for their trek across the island.

About half an hour later, they set off. Brody had tried asking Rose why they were going there and if the destination was her home or where her people were, but he couldn't make himself understood and he had a hard time interpreting any gestures she did give in reply. She mostly smiled at him as if she was amused by his chattering. The journey had started with Rose pulling her cart, but Brody had quickly taken it from her, like a dutiful boyfriend. Rose wasn't used to this kind of standard gallantry and she was immensely touched by it. She led the way with Brody following, both of them privately revelling in the exquisite tenderness that was going on between them.

# CHAPTER SIX
# "EDEN"

Julianne and the group of survivors had been making their own trek since the sun had come up that morning. Julianne stopped walking as they reached a huge hedge wall that went as far as the horizon in both directions.

"We're here," she told the group.

The group all made various noises and looked around.

"It's a hedge," Mrs. LaGrance said.

"Yes. The hedge surrounds the garden. There is an entrance about a mile that way," Julianne told them before turning and walking alongside the hedge-wall. She didn't wait for the others to follow, she just expected that they would. And they did.

Bridie ran a little ahead of the others to catch up with Julianne. "What are we going to find in there?"

Julianne seemed to hesitate. It was the first time Bridie had seen any kind of reluctance in Julianne's demeanour. "The first man," she eventually said.

Bridie stopped walking for a moment at the enormity of Julianne's simple answer. She then jogged to catch up with the immortal woman again. "The first man?"

"Yes, and the second man," Julianne stated.

Bridie nodded. "What about the third man? Am I going to meet Orson Welles?" she joked in reference to the movie, The Third Man.

"Orson Welles?" Julianne asked. "Is he another one of your religious figures?"

Bridie laughed. "To some of us, yes."

"Well, there was a third man, but he was banished."

"Why was he banished?" Bridie asked.

"He invented sex."

Bridie stopped walking for the second time in their conversation. After a few seconds of contemplation, Bridie jogged forwards again. "He invented sex? And that made him eligible for banishment?"

"Yes. With his invention of sex, he also created enhanced notions of hedonism, jealousy, paranoia, hatred, wantonness, guilt and, of course, lust. Sex has also created a new kind of violence and can be used as the ultimate form of abuse."

Bridie shrugged. "Yeah, but it feels great when you get it right."

"I wouldn't know."

"Seriously? You've never had sex?" Bridie asked, grinning.

"Of course I haven't. I'm not a barbarian."

Bridie was offended on behalf of the human race by Julianne's dismissive attitude. She decided to join the others again and leave Julianne ahead of the group. Everybody was generally too tired to talk, even though they all had plenty to talk about. There was also, largely, still a reluctance within the group for them to look at each other since they were all naked. Privately, nobody minded that they were all naked, but having been brought up in a society that hid nakedness, it still jarred at their sensibilities to be around it.

As they walked in silence, a calamitous sound echoed through the air. It was the sound of a tremendous roar – the roar of a large creature somewhere in the distance. Bridie decided to run ahead and join Julianne again.

"What was that noise?"

"It's nothing to worry about," Julianne replied. "It's just the T-Rex."

"T-Rex?" Bridie cried.

"Say that again," said Condy who had followed Bridie to the front with Julianne.

"We have a T-Rex!" Julianne explained.

Bridie laughed. "Oh my God! It's just like Jurassic Park!"

Julianne stopped walking and turned to look at Bridie. "It's nothing like Jurassic Park," she said before returning on her journey.

"Wait!" said Bridie with surprise. "You've heard of Jurassic Park? You haven't heard of Jesus Christ, but you've heard of Jurassic Park?"

"Of course," Julianne said matter-of-factly. "Everyone's heard of Jurassic Park."

"Unbelievable."

Something was coming up ahead, or to be more accurate, something was stationary ahead and the group were coming upon it. There was an obvious gap in the hedge they were following, some distance before them. As they approached it, it became more obvious that it was a gate, a very large gate, either made of, or painted, gold. When Julianne reached the gate, she paused. She seemed hesitant and awestruck, or maybe it was nostalgic. She had returned home after who-knows how long, probably millions of years, and that would be enough to give anyone pause. After a few moments, she got over it and pushed at the gate. The two magnificent doors easily swung open revealing a winding path heading far into the beautiful and well kept garden.

Julianne turned to face the group, and with a flushed face, gave the following speech. “Come on,” she said and headed into the garden. Condy, Bridie, Zachary, Mrs. LaGrance, Edmond, the captain and the rest of the crew went into the garden after her, despite their reservations. The main feature of the garden that compelled them to enter and ignore any perceived dangers, was that the garden was astonishing. All the plant-life was oversized and bursting with colour, as if someone had turned the saturation up to maximum. There were flowers of all hues, trees of all shapes and grasses of all lengths swaying in the gentle breeze. The path they were following gradually curved to the right and led them towards a series of small buildings which the group would all have described as man-made if they hadn’t become accustomed to the idea that immortals lived on this island and they perhaps shouldn’t be described as ‘man’. As they approached the first of the buildings, they all became aware of somebody whistling. Julianne suddenly stopped still and waved her hand behind her as an indication for the group to stay still for the moment.

“What is it?” Mrs. LaGrance whispered.

Julianne stayed absolutely still for a few seconds. “It’s Adam.”

This caused consternation among the group which Julianne noisily shushed. The whistling stopped and it was clear that the whistler had heard either the consternation or the shush. A few moments later, a naked man came out of the hut. He had a supremely confident demeanour and didn't appear remotely startled or concerned with the group's presence. Other than that, he was something of a disappointment. Considering he was supposed to be *the* Adam and an immortal, he had an average body and a plain face

"Julianne," he warmly greeted his friend.

"Adam," Julianne reflected. They stood staring at each other for a little while before Julianne ran up to Adam and threw her arms around his neck. She was breathing heavily, as if she was suffering an anxiety attack.

"Hey, hey," Adam said soothingly, putting his hands on her waist. "Hey, hey, hey."

The members of the group all glanced at each other, surprised by this uncharacteristic emotional outburst by Julianne. She had been nothing but intemperate since they had met her. Clearly she had been successfully hiding her feelings behind a poker face.

Julianne pulled away from Adam and wiped a single tear from one of her eyes. "Why didn't you come and find me?"

Adam shook his head. "You know we couldn't," he simply replied. "But I had faith that you would be found by the people."

Condy leaned in close to Bridie's ear while they all watched the reunion. "How's he speaking English?"

Bridie considered the question and realised it was baffling. When they had first met Julianne, she had used some kind of telepathy to learn their language, so how did Adam know the language?

"I learned your language from Julianne… just now," Adam answered.

Bridie looked up at Adam in surprise. He was looking directly at her.

"But never mind these silly details," Adam went on to say. "I should introduce myself. I am Adam. I am the first man."

Everybody in the group stared blankly at Adam. "What exactly does that mean?" Mrs. LaGrance boldly asked.

"You do know what first means, right?" Adam asked her.

"Of course, but…"

"I am the original of your species. I am the template of your race. I am the ideal specimen from which your variety was derived. I created mortal man, based on my own image, and then, to accompany man, I invented woman, an improvement on the original."

"Improvement?" Bridie asked with a smile.

"Certainly," Adam confirmed. "Would you like to meet the first woman?"

"You mean, it's not Julianne?" Zachary asked.

Julianne looked away, showing clear signs of jealousy.

"Julianne is a member of my family and I love her very much, but she was not the first woman. Julianne was…" Adam paused, searching for the right word. He looked into Julianne's eyes. "She was an experiment, but… things didn't work out." As he said this, Adam was rubbing Julianne's upper arm affectionately.

"So, who is the first woman?" the captain asked.

Adam smiled, and then strode over to the hut next to his. He leaned inside and, even though nobody could see his face, they could tell he was talking to somebody. The conversation went on for just a few seconds, and then Adam leaned back out of the hut. He reached back inside to assist the emergence of the first woman.

The woman who stepped out of the hut and then sauntered elegantly towards the group was the most stunning specimen of femininity anybody had ever seen. She had vibrant, flowing blood-red hair, comely brown eyes, perfect features and freckles. Her proportions were so balanced they could only have been calculated. She was clearly the meticulous creation of a genius and not the product of chaos. Every man in the group was mesmerised.

"This is Sabrina," Adam said.

"Hi," said all the men.

Sabrina simply smiled. The human women all tutted.

"I have a question?" Bridie piped up.

Adam set his eyes upon her. "Yes?"

"Julianne told me she had never had sex."

"That's correct."

"And the way she said it implied that none of the immortals have sex."

"That's right," Adam confirmed. "Sex was Benedict's idea."

"He was the one who was banished?" Bridie asked, remembering what Julianne had told her.

"Correct."

"So, my question is this," Bridie went on. "If none of the immortals have sex, then why do you have a dick?"

A few members of the group chuckled at this brusque enquiry. Adam looked down at his physique and contemplated the question. He seemed either reluctant or unable to answer.

"I mean," Bridie continued before Adam got around to answering, "Julianne told us that immortals don't consume food and, therefore, don't defecate or urinate, so it can't even be for that."

Adam considered the question a little longer before giving the single word answer, "Decoration."

"Decoration?" Bridie exclaimed. "Sorry, Adam, you might have the body of a god, but even *your* cock isn't exactly something I'd keep on the mantlepiece."

A strange shadow seemed to cast itself over Adam's face and he approached Bridie menacingly. "I advise more caution in your tone, young lady. I created you and you ought to have more respect."

Seeing Bridie's face quiver at Adam's parental tone, Zachary stepped in between Adam and Bridie. He put on the bravest, toughest face he could muster. "Leave her alone."

Adam examined Zachary's countenance. He was impressed enough to give a little smile. The shadow over his face disappeared. "Good for you."

Zachary felt more than a little patronised.

"What's your name?" Adam then asked him.

"Zachary."

"Well done, Zachary. You're a credit to your species."

Adam turned and strode back to his spot between Sabrina and Julianne. "I'm sure you have many more questions, and so I suggest you freshen up, have something to eat and we will all gather around the rainbow table in an hour, and we will go over everything."

All the mortals looked around at each other. The whole situation had been developing so quickly that none of them had really given themselves chance to let anything sink in. Everything felt dreamlike for the time being. The general unspoken consensus among the group was to accept Adam's suggestion.

"But, before that, I have one more person for you to meet," Adam said with a beam of pride in his voice. "The one I couldn't have done any of this without. My life-long, ever-loving partner."

A small gasp echoed around the group, followed by whispers of anticipation. Without exception, the whispers all said "Eve,"

Adam walked over to another nearby hut and stood by it. "I would like you all to greet the love of my life…"

From the hut, a figure emerged. The figure belonged to a tall, blonde, good-looking man.

"Everyone, say hello to Steve."

CHAPTER SEVEN
"CEREMONY"

It had been a few hours of trekking through the wilderness for Brody and Rose. Rose had occasionally offered to take the burden of the cart from Brody, but Brody was insistent that he wanted to carry it for her. She smiled happily each time, and Brody got the impression that towards the end, she was only asking so that she could feel the warmth of his gallantry. He didn't mind if that was her reason. He liked the feeling it gave him too.

The couple were climbing a shallow incline surrounded by bushes and scattered with trees. It wasn't exactly like a typical forest, there was too much visibility, but there was a distinct sensation of being surrounded to be felt. The path they were following was a long, straight trail of flattened grass as though the journey had been taken many times before. At one point, Rose suddenly stopped walking and froze. Her demeanour indicated that she had heard something. She held her arm out backwards towards Brody who was following, and he froze too.

"What's wrong?" he whispered.

Rose turned to look at him and she put her finger to her lips. She looked a little afraid, but also a little exhilarated. After a few moments of silent stillness, they both heard a twig snapping. Brody and Rose both sharply turned their heads in the same direction to see a large woolly creature racing towards them. The creature resembled a boar but it was much fluffier than the ones Brody had seen on the television, and it had a very long tail that whipped about in the air, like a cowboy's lasso. With lightning speed Rose went to the cart and produced a huge blade which she brandished with impressive skill. The boar was heading directly for Rose which instilled in Brody an uncharacteristic and overwhelming sense of protectiveness. Before he could stop himself, not that he would have done, Brody dropped the cart and leapt in front of Rose to intercept the boar. He had only just found her, he couldn't lose her already. With surprising strength (although it wasn't all that surprising considering how she had virtually ravished him on the beach), Rose pushed Brody aside in order to take on the boar herself. Brody fell to the ground but quickly got onto all fours just in time to see the boar slightly change direction and head towards him. Rose let out a shriek of horror, and she plunged the blade into the beast's back just as it reached Brody. The boy was struck by the monstrous boar enough to send him rolling painfully into the grass, where he lifted his head up to see Rose repeatedly plunging the blade into the struggling boar's torso until the furry furious animal ceased struggling and lay lifeless beside her. Rose was splattered with the boar's blood, and as soon as she was certain the boar was dead, she clambered over to Brody to make sure he was okay. She put her bloody hand tenderly on his cheek and stared into his eyes looking for signs of pain. Brody managed to display a smile which seemed to ease her concern. She then started kissing him repeatedly all over his face until their lips locked together and they embraced lustfully for a while. Brody was sensing from her that she was expressing gratitude, even delight, at the fact that he had tried to protect her from the boar even though she had a weapon and he didn't. She pushed him down on the grass and climbed on top of him again. Brody didn't struggle or object or resist. He was so in love with this mystery mute girl, that he had become her slave. They had rampant, furious sex while wiping boar's blood all over each other from what had been splashed on Rose's skin. Humping away like this, in the afternoon, outdoors, covered in sacrificial blood was one of the most erotic moments of Brody's life.

After their steamy distraction, Rose and Brody took a few minutes, cuddling, to catch their breaths before Rose, with gourmet skill, skinned the boar for its meat. She found two adequate sticks and handed them to Brody to see if he knew what to do with them. He tentatively rubbed them together while giving Rose a look begging approval. Rose shook her head with a smirk and took the sticks from him. Within minutes she had a fire burning and was cooking the strips of boar meat for their lunch. While the boar meat cooked, Rose began to dance once more. This time the dance had a more curvy nature with lots of sweeping arms and kicking legs. It seemed to Brody it was some kind of cooking ritual dance. She encouraged him to join in and once again, he did his best. Rose was turning out to be an excellent dance teacher because, with her tuition, he picked it up quickly. Once the meat was well cooked, Rose laid it all on one of the thin stone slabs she kept in her cart, and she offered some of the food to Brody. Brody happily took a strip of the meat, shuffled a little closer to her and held it to her mouth.

Rose smiled, opened her mouth and accepted the food from him. Brody and Rose fed each other for the rest of the meal. It was romantic and affectionate, and it bonded them some more, even though their bond had been obvious and virtually impenetrable from the moment they had first looked into each other's eyes.

After they had finished eating, they packed up the cart and continued on their journey. As they trekked on, the surrounding forest became thicker. It seemed to be getting dark but that was just an illusion created by the density of the trees. Brody noticed that Rose had slowed down considerably over the last few minutes and she had adopted a stooped, cautious stance as she went. Brody stayed close behind her, in one way pleased about the reduced speed because he was still pulling the cart, but otherwise disturbed by the boding anticipation her actions instilled. Eventually, Rose stopped walking altogether and Brody stood beside her, carefully putting the cart down. It wasn't exactly dark in the forest, but it was overcast and shadowy enough to make them unsure of what might be lurking ahead. Rose was clearly sensing or expecting something to be out there. Brody watched Rose's face as she scanned the area. She was focussed and alert, like a hunter. Brody was so turned on by her like this that he almost forgot to be afraid of whatever it was she was anticipating. Rose didn't look at Brody because she was busy, but she took hold of his hand to let him know she wasn't ignoring him. She was protecting them both. Brody's manhood was a little bruised at knowing Rose was the protector of the two of them, but she was so sexy like this, that he got over it.

Rose stopped breathing and consequently, so did Brody. In the silence, Brody heard footsteps. They were clearly human footsteps, and he turned in the direction of the sound. Rose was already looking that way. A naked man was approaching them. He was about Brody's age, early twenties. His facial expression was stern, but not menacing. As he closed on them, Rose let go of Brody's hand and her demeanour relaxed from hunter to something more civilised, almost authoritative, even commanding. The man approaching, once he was sure he recognised Rose, fell down onto one knee and bowed his head. Brody watched with awe at the genuflecting man realising there was much more to Rose than just being a mute hunter. The more he thought about it, the more it made sense. Rose was a hunter, but she wasn't a savage. The tenderness he had experienced with her demonstrated something much more sophisticated and civilised. Rose walked regally over to the kneeling man and placed her hand on his bowed head. When she removed her hand, the man rose. She leaned in and kissed him briefly on the nose. Brody smiled, pleased with himself that he had already discerned that the nose-kiss was a greeting of her people. The man kissed Rose's nose in response, and then he stepped back with his head slightly tilted down as if to demonstrate subordination. Rose turned to look at Brody and held out her hand for him to take. Brody, assuming a role similar to the man they had just met, took her hand but slightly bowed his head to demonstrate a willingness to be her subordinate. Rose put her free hand under his chin and lifted his head up, gently shaking her head in order to convey to Brody that he wasn't expected to do that, and that he was her equal.

"Who are you?" he asked her out of wonder and esteem for what he was witnessing.

As Brody spoke the words, the bowing man looked up, startled. Rose had anticipated the man's reaction and immediately held her hand out to him, putting her index finger supine which appeared to be an assertion that the man shouldn't be alarmed. The man accepted Rose's signal and he bowed his head once again. Rose then clicked her fingers and the man looked upon her clearly waiting for her next communication. Rose turned to Brody and kissed him on the lips with glorious, comforting tenderness. Brody returned the kiss with requited affection, but he had the feeling that this kiss was more of a demonstration than an act of love. When they pulled away from the kiss, the man was staring at them with such astonishment that Brody couldn't help but feel like he was in trouble. Rose was clearly something akin to royalty to this man and it made Brody feel like he might be committing sacrilege. The man stepped towards Brody, examined his face studiously, and then the man dropped down onto one knee before Brody, bowing his head once again. Brody watched the man with confusion, and he looked to Rose for some kind of explanation. Rose's smile made Brody feel safe, like she was protecting him once again. He absolutely trusted her, and he genuinely didn't know if it was because he could trust her or if he wanted to. Either way, he wilfully belonged to her. The bowing man stayed in his position. Rose gestured that Brody should put his hand on the man's head to release him from his sycophancy. Brody touched the man's head tentatively and the man, as if released from his servitude, rose to his feet and gave Brody a respectful expression. Brody appreciated the man's response, but he didn't really understand it. It seemed that the man worshipped Rose (which was something Brody did understand), but he couldn't fathom why her kiss had made the man partisan to him as well.

"Thank you," Brody said because he felt like he should say something even though he knew that the words didn't mean anything to the man.

Rose made some gestures to the man. Brody interpreted her simple gestures as being, roughly, 'let's go'. The man put his two little fingers in his mouth and chimed a very loud whistle. A small number of other men and women emerged from the trees around them, and they all approached Rose and Brody with the same level of admiration as Brody had seen in the man they had just met. Brody decided he would name the man Saturday, which he thought was kind of funny. The emerging crowd all recognised Rose and went down on their knees to offer their respects and admiration for her. This lasted only a few moments and then the crowd arranged themselves in a line in front of Brody and Rose. Brody counted seven people altogether, or nine with him and Rose. The seven who were lined up in front of them, broke into an elaborate and well coordinated dance that lasted about a minute. Brody watched with awe as it struck him that dance was clearly a way for this culture to communicate. As the dance finished, five of the group gathered around Brody and Rose in a protective circle. Saturday turned and led the way.

The remaining member of the group took the rear and pulled Rose's cart. Rose took Brody's hand and they followed Saturday's lead. The circle of protectors moved along with them keeping the circle intact. As they walked, Brody looked at Rose in a new light. He still adored her, but the way her people treated her made him nervous. He hadn't realised he was falling in love with royalty, or whatever the equivalent is in their society. And then he thought, maybe it was something else. Maybe she was more like a celebrity. Maybe she was famous among her people because of an enormous talent she had. Perhaps she was an actress, or an artist or a singer…

"No, not a singer," Brody thought aloud, "these people are mute."

Many of the group looked at him as he spoke, but nobody stopped moving. Brody realised he had spoken his thoughts aloud again while he was lost in thought. He really had to stop doing that.

After about half an hour of travelling, the group arrived at their destination. It was an enormous clearing, a huge flat plain of land littered with primitive looking huts and elemental buildings. Milling around these buildings were collections of naked humans, bustling about, exercising their community, and going about their everyday business. As Brody, Rose and their group emerged from the surrounding overgrowth, their presence was noticed by the community, and consternation erupted quickly. It was a strange thing for Brody to witness. The consternation was mute but palpable. The previously milling around population evolved into a collectively curious and relieved people. They were relieved to see their princess again, and they ran towards the travellers, each of them stooping to their knees in reverence of Rose's return as they became close enough to determine that it was her. Before long, Brody and Rose were left the only ones standing, surrounded by a numerous throng of kneeling, worshipping admirers. The consternation soon descended into a steady, rhythmic, swaying obeisance towards Rose. Brody observed the reverence of her people and he was impressed with the humility with which she received their reverence. Rose wasn't acting like a spoiled aristocracy puppet, or like a privileged, self-important luminary. Instead, she walked among her people, gesturing them to rise from their self-belittlement and to stand beside her. Brody had no idea if he had the right, but nevertheless, he was proud of her for her constraint. It was clear to Brody that the reason they worshipped Rose so absolutely was exactly because she didn't consider herself more important than they were. They loved her, not because she was important, but because she had position and she didn't allow it to corrupt her. And Brody loved her for that reason too. Once the people had risen to their feet, Brody approached Rose and before he could embrace her or take her hand, she reached back and found his hand first.

"Our princess has returned!" a voice cried out from the crowd.

Nobody was more surprised than Brody. Everybody turned to observe the owner of the voice emerging from a large tent in the middle of the village. When Brody looked at the man, his first impression was that the man's eyes were too close together. Apart from that, Brody saw something familiar and likeable about the man.

Rose approached the speaking man, urging Brody to follow her by not letting go of his hand, and then they were standing with him. Rose looked at Brody and made a gesture with her hand, rippling near her mouth, that Brody discerned as being a cue for him to talk.

Brody looked at the man who had spoken. “Hello,” he said.

The man paused for a moment and then smiled. “Hello,” he said in return. “My name is Benedict.”

Benedict leaned forward and kissed Brody on the nose, which Brody was now certain was their way of greeting. Brody returned the gesture.

“My name is Brody,” he told Benedict.

Benedict hesitated, giving his next expression some consideration. “Welcome to our village, Brody,” he eventually said. “What brings you here?”

Brody found himself confounded by the sudden presence of somebody who wasn’t only speaking, but speaking English. “I came here on a ship. It sank, and I think Rose saved me.”

“Rose?”

Brody looked at Rose to indicate he was referencing her. “I don’t know if she has a name, but it’s the name I gave her.”

“It’s a pretty name,” Benedict said. “It suits her. Their people don’t have names. They don’t have any language”

“Who is she?”

Benedict grinned. "She was elected their queen, their protector. They chose her because she is the best of them."

"Yeah," Brody agreed. "I'm crazy about her."

Rose chose this moment to interrupt their conversation. She took Benedict's face in her hand and moved him to watch her. Benedict followed her loyally. Rose stared at Benedict for a few moments in order to ascertain his attention, and then she focussed her gaze on Brody before giving him one of the most passionate kisses his lips had ever been lucky enough to receive. The kiss endured mutually and there were gasps from the observing crowd, and a look of awe from Benedict. When the kiss ended, Brody was out of breath, and out of context. Benedict's face froze. Brody's mind reeled with confusion.

"Did I do something wrong?" he asked. "Is kissing Rose a sin or something?"

Benedict shook his head. "No," he answered simply. "But I'm not sure you've understood the gravity of this act. In their culture… in our culture, for a man and woman to kiss on the lips…" Benedict hesitated because he was aware that Brody might not have been fully consensual about the implications of kissing Rose, "…for a man and a woman to kiss on the lips is a declaration of marriage."

Brody was understandably staggered by this information. "Oh," he said. "I… I didn't know that," he stuttered. Without being conscious of it, he let go of Rose's hand. Rose looked up at him, startled. "I'm sorry, I didn't realise that a kiss meant so much to you. I thought it was just a kiss… it was only a kiss."

"Did you mate with her?"

Brody paused. "Okay, yes, we did that, too."

"Then the marriage was consummated."

Brody looked Rose in her eyes. His affection for her was enormous, but this news was shattering. He watched her expression fall from confident and happy, to confused and lost. It almost broke his heart.

"Please, Benedict, please, is there any way I can communicate to her that I didn't understand? I didn't know I was marrying her."

Benedict's facial expression had become extremely stern. "I can show her," Benedict told him, and then he gently turned Rose's face to confront his. He stared at her for a few moments and then she let out a yelp and pushed him away from her.

"Rose," Brody blurted out, putting his hand on her arm to comfort her. She slapped his hand away with scorned force, glanced briefly into his eyes so he could see her rage, and then she ran away from the scene, making a sustained wailing sound as she departed.

Brody attempted to go after her, but Benedict stopped him. "You've broken her heart. Let her go and heal."

"I made a mistake," Brody said passionately.

"It isn't your fault. It's nobody's fault. It was the result of two different cultures misunderstanding…"

"That isn't what I meant," Brody interrupted, and he pulled himself free of Benedict's grip to go in pursuit of his wife.

When Brody found Rose, she was lying on her side on the bank of a stream, sobbing uncontrollably. Brody couldn't bear to see her this way, and he ran over to her. When she heard him approach, she stifled her tears as much as she could, but she didn't move or turn to look at him. Brody knelt down behind her and very gently put his hand on her waist.

"Rose… I'm sorry."

Rose continued to remain still. The feel of his touch and the sound of his voice were a comfort, but it wasn't enough to placate her fury. She turned quickly over and punched Brody on the chest. Her blow was surprisingly forceful, throwing Brody onto his back, and then she was on top of him, beating at his chest with bounteous ferocity. Brody tried to fight her off, but her outrage made her so strong. When she could see that she was really hurting him, Rose backed away looking regretful but still indignant. Her rampancy was only a little quelled. Brody clamoured painfully to his feet and held out his arm as a request for her to calm down. They both stood, panting for a few moments before Brody put his arm down and he slowly approached her. Rose snarled at him as a warning not to get any closer. Brody ignored it and shuffled another couple of tentative steps towards her. Rose's emotions had converted into a kind of sulking, lip quivering mope. When Brody was close enough for her to touch him, she half-heartedly pushed him away. Brody persevered through her resistance and took a step closer, putting his arms around her waist. Rose placed her fists on his chest and made a quarter-hearted effort to push him away. She hadn't looked him in the eye, until now. Brody smiled. Rose didn't. She felt betrayed. Brody thought about the first time she had kissed him, how she had looked nervous and tentative the moments before. It all made sense now. When he had tried to kiss her first, she had thought it was a proposal, and then she had fidgeted and poured over the idea. And then she had kissed him. She had agreed to marry him. Brody brushed Rose's hair from her eyes, and they stared at each other for an eternity. Rose's face had her broken heart all over it.

"I love you," he said, and Rose smiled. She hadn't understood him, obviously, but the tone of his voice told her the sentiment.

Brody leaned in towards her lips and, at first, Rose pulled back to resist. Brody didn't want to force or influence her decision. He simply wanted her to realise that this time he was asking her to be his wife, that this time he understood what he was doing. Brody pulled back, to give her time to consider his proposal. A moment later, she stuck her tongue down his throat, and soon after, they were consummating the marriage once again.

# CHAPTER EIGHT
# "T-REX"

On the other side of the island, Bridie's team were in the middle of a conference with Adam, Steve, Sabrina and Julianne. They were sitting at what Adam had called the rainbow table. It was named this simply because it was a huge round table with a rainbow painted on it. Surrounding the table was a continuous circular bench which everyone in the group had parked themselves on. The table was out in the open air, in the centre of the immortals' living area. The natural beauty surrounding them was delicious. Evidently, the table was their discussion centre.

"So, it's Adam and Steve after all," Mrs. LaGrance said to the immortals. "This isn't going to go down well back home."

"Except with the atheists," suggested Zachary.

"Why do you have such a large table when there were only four of you to sit at it?" Bridie asked.

"There were five of us originally with Benedict," Steve replied.

"That's right," Adam concurred, "but the main reason the table is so large is because we expected that, over time, there would be many more members of our group."

"But things didn't work out that way," Julianne added.

"Look," the captain said, "we're getting little bits of information here, but we're not really learning anything about you people."

"What would you like to know?"

"Well," the captain began, "Okay, firstly, what's your background? Where did you people come from? Where were you born or created or whatever happened?"

"You mortals, you assume that because you begin and end, that everything else does as well. Some things, like myself and Steve, simply always are. You are four-dimensional beings who exist in height, width, depth and time. We have only three dimensions. We are aware of the existence of time, and we even travel in it, we simply aren't affected by it. We don't age and we can't be damaged. We also aren't susceptible to such concepts as boredom or nostalgia. These notions can only exist where time is a factor."

Condy put her hand up in the air out of respect. Adam smiled. "Just talk, Condy. There's no need to be so polite."

Condy put her hand down. "If you don't exist in time, does that mean you can't fall in love? Because, surely, that's something that takes time to happen."

Everybody turned to Adam in anticipation. This was an interesting question. "You are correct, Condy. We cannot fall in love, but that doesn't mean that we don't love. I love Steve and Sabrina and Julianne and even Benedict, despite the fact that I was compelled to banish him. I also love all of you. You see, when you don't exist in time, love is your default feeling. You feel love for everything and everybody. It's the threat of eventual, inevitable death that causes humans to be paranoid and desperate and suspicious because you have everything to lose. I do envy you."

"You envy us because we're mortal?" Bridie asked incredulously.

"Yes, very much so," Adam replied. The other immortals at the table nodded in agreement. "I have no idea what it's like to fall in love. Tell me what it's like."

The mortals at the table looked at each other, waiting for someone to find a way of describing it. "It's like losing your mind," Edmund said, and he looked across at Condy. "But it's worth it."

Condy smiled at Edmund, but she was honestly embarrassed at his implication that his falling in love description had anything to do with her.

"Falling in love is about believing in perfection," Bridie suggested. "When I fell in love with Brody," she continued, but was forced to pause as she said his name out of fear that she would probably never see him again. "When I fell in love with Brody, we had already been friends for years. I knew all his faults already, and yet, when I fell in love with him, I saw him as being perfect. After the honeymoon period ended, all I could see were his flaws, and we didn't like each other very much."

"How complicated," Adam observed gleefully.

"But then we broke up, and he became my best friend again."

People smiled at the happy ending of Bridie's story. "And where is he now?" Adam asked, naively.

"He's… gone. He was with us on our ship. He never came out of the water," Bridie morosely imparted.

Adam's facial expression glazed over slightly for a moment and then he came back to the group. "He's with Benedict."

Bridie's ears pricked up and she stared at Adam. "What?"

"He's with Benedict. One of Benedict's refugees found him."

Bridie put her hand to her mouth and she welled up slightly. "How do you know?"

"Oh, mortals don't have telepathy, do they?"

Everybody automatically shook their heads. "You read our minds," Condy joked. Nobody realised it was a joke.

"Are you sure? Brody's alive?"

Adam nodded. He almost looked hurt that Bridie had to ask for confirmation. "Trust me, he's on the other side of the island with Benedict's people."

The captain decided it was time to get some real answers, again. "So, who is this Benedict? And why did you banish him?"

"I told you," Julianne interjected. "He invented sex for pleasure, and with sex came corruption, selfishness and greed. Sex was the worst thing that could happen to the humans."

"Don't knock what you haven't tried," Bridie suggested.

"Yes," Adam said. "We decided to banish Benedict for his obsession with sex in general, and his insistence that we make sexual coupling the ultimate pleasure in the make-up of the human race. Benedict was convinced that by making reproduction pleasurable, it would ensure the survival of the mortals. I had rejected the idea because I anticipated such pleasure would be a distraction from spiritual progress and could even become a dangerous weapon which would be inevitably susceptible to abuse."

"I think you were both right," Zachary said. "But I have to say, given the options, that the upsides to sex far outweigh the downsides. It seems to me that this Benedict made a mistake in your eyes, but to banish him for that seems extremely… extreme."

Adam nodded. "There were other factors."

Bridie was starting to get emotional at the way the conversation was drifting from what she thought was important. "Can you take us to Benedict?" she asked. "Can you take me to find Brody. He's my best friend. I'd like to see him again."

"That may be difficult," Adam said. "Benedict has always been volatile."

"Can we just go back to something you said earlier?" the captain asked. "You said that you and Steve weren't created. Does that mean that Julianne and Sabrina were?"

"Yes," Adam concurred. "Me and Benedict had observed that in the animal kingdom there were almost always a male gender and a female gender, whereas we immortals were solely male. We decided to engineer a female version of ourselves, but Benedict and I disagreed on many of the details, so we each created a female."

"Julianne and Sabrina," Zachary supposed.

"Of course. I created Sabrina, and Benedict created Julianne. Benedict was always fascinated by the animal concept of sex. His idea was to create a female mate for himself."

"Like in Weird Science," Bridie suggested.

"I have no idea what that is," Adam coldly replied before carrying on. "But Benedict found himself unable to perform the sexual act with Julianne."

"Benedict concluded that as I was his creation," Julianne elaborated, "I was technically his daughter which explained why our sexual coupling was repugnant to us. It gave us a sensation of… I can't seem to find the word…"

"I think the word you're looking for is 'ew'," Bridie suggested.

"Yes, that's exactly the correct modern colloquial expression."

"And the next problem was that Benedict seemed to have a sexual interest in me instead," Sabrina explained. "We couldn't understand why."

All the mortal men at the table snorted at this remark. Even some of the woman did.

"You people don't understand sex at all do you?" Zachary observed.

Adam didn't reply for a few moments. "Of course we do."

"It's how you make offspring," Sabrina stated.

"Anyway, to tie up the story," Adam went on, "Benedict persuaded us that the key was sexuality and mortality, so we created mortals. The first batch were flawed. They were virtually incapable of mastering language, and they had no concept of growth. They didn't know how to learn. They had a healthy sexual appetite and they bred, but we discovered that each female could only give birth once or twice at the most, and some of them were sterile, so they didn't flourish. Each generation equalled the previous and their numbers remained the same. Death rates equalled birth rates. And there were a number of other problems, so we made a second batch, fixing all these problems – multiple births, adapting to their surroundings, speech, etc. This second batch was much more successful and before we knew it, they were spreading like a disease."

"We had to get them off the island," Steve continued. "We knew that there was plenty of space in the outside world, so we committed a mendacity."

"A what?" Edmund asked.

"A lie," Julianne translated. "We told the second-tier humans that a great flood was coming and that they had to build an enormous vessel to carry them to safer lands."

The humans at the rainbow table shuddered slightly. "An arc?" Condy said.

"I suppose so," Julianne agreed.

"So, we packed them all onto the 'arc' and sent them safely away," Sabrina added.

"And then we decided to extend natural defences up around our island to prevent the humans from returning," Adam said. "The first-tier humans, the mutes, remained with us. My suggestion was to destroy them, but I was outvoted."

"Destroy them?" Condy exclaimed. "You can't go around extinguishing life on a whim. Who do you think you are?"

"He thinks he's a god," Mrs. LaGrance suggested. "And he kind of is."

"I thought it would be kinder to extinguish them rather than condemn them to their limited lives.

Benedict was always too attached to our subjects, and he insisted we let them live."

"I was loyal to Adam," Steve said. "I voted for the extinction of the first-tiers."

"You mean genocide!" Condy angrily retorted.

"I mean mercy."

"Me and Sabrina voted for their survival," Julianne added.

"Good for you, girls," Condy proudly endorsed.

"Shouldn't it be 'Sabrina and I', grammatically speaking?" one of the other members of the crew asked smugly.

"Oh, grow up!"

"So, we gave the first-tiers their own patch of land on the other side of the island and left them alone, knowing that they would never stray back here because they had no sense of curiosity," Steve relayed.

"It was at this time, I started to become concerned with Benedict's obsession," Adam said. "His time with the humans had exacerbated his fascination with sex, and he was becoming increasingly and alarmingly attentive towards Sabrina."

"He was a pest," Sabrina said. "At first, it was charming, but then it became uncomfortable. He actually wanted to perform sex with me."

"Imagine that," Zachary sarcastically quipped. Mrs. LaGrance jealously slapped him on the arm.

"Eventually, he became erratic and unmanageable. As a committee we agreed he should be banished from the island. We built a capsule to transport him to the outside world."

"But he trickled me into getting into the capsule instead," Julianne continued. "And that's why you found me buried in the sand."

"We took Benedict to the other side of the island, brainwashed him, and returned here. Since then, he has been with the first-tiers. He has been helping the mute humans to grow a little and have a better life. He has been with them for many generations now, and he has guided them to respect tradition, ceremony, love and family. They have even developed rudimentary tools and weapons for survival."

"Meanwhile, in the rest of the world," Steve added, "you second-tiers have almost destroyed the planet with your creativity."

"And now that Julianne is back, we can continue with our plans," Adam revealed.

"Plans?" Condy asked. The rest of the humans around the table were consumed with nervous curiosity.

"Yes," Adam answered. "We plan to introduce a third tier of humans."

"A new race. One that is less motivated by greed and self-preservation, but equally able to grow and adapt to surroundings. We've designed a middle ground between the passive first-tier and the aggressive second-tier."

"Oh, a sort of passive-aggressive race, then?" Condy dubiously supposed.

"Yes," Adam concurred.

"Unfortunately," Steve gravely interjected, "this time, it will mean the eradication of the second-tiers."

Steve's blasé statement caused a damning pall to descend upon them all. The humans looked around at each other wondering if they had all heard the same thing.

"You don't mean that?" Bridie asked.

"You're going to wipe us out?" Edmund said.

"Yes," Adam confirmed. "But you nine are welcome to remain here under our protection."

"You're not destroying mankind, will-nilly. That's pure evil!" Condy chided.

"You can't create life and then just destroy it because you don't like the life that you created," Zachary said.

"Yes, I can," Adam insisted with a cold demeanour.

The humans had run out of things to say, and they sat in stunned silence.

Adam started to laugh, and he was then followed by Julianne, Sabrina and Steve. Something was extremely funny to them, and the rest of the group watched befuddled, as the immortals cachinnated exaggeratedly.

"I'm just kidding!" Adam coughed through his laughter. "We wanted to see how you would react."

The stunned silence the humans had shared a moment ago changed into a whole new stunned silence, although a couple of them grinned slightly, but mostly out of relief rather than amusement.

"We are pleased to see that you were appalled," Steve told them. "Since we sent your species out into your world, we have been aware of your general behaviour."

"The big things," Adam said. "Your wars, mainly, so we were concerned that you were only violent. It is rewarding to see how compassionate you can be."

The silence from the humans endured, so Bridie decided it was a good opportunity to speak about an unresolved issue. "So, now we're all friends, can we go and find Brody?"

Adam nodded. "Fortunately for everybody, our goals seem to coincide. Our intention is to reunite all the survivors of your accident and send you back to the world you came from. There is no place for you here. You need to go back to your people, but I implore you not to reveal anything of this island to the rest of your world. They will not be able to find it, and if they do believe you, it will only cause chaos among your scientists and religious groups, and panic among your people."

Most of the humans around the table considered this to be reasonable. All except one. "Mr, Adam," Mrs. LaGrance began, "we have spent a great deal of our money and resources and time getting to this island. Some of our people have made the ultimate sacrifice on our journey. Do you really expect us to return home with nothing to show for it?"

Adam considered Mrs. LaGrance's question. "Yes, I do."

"I can't agree to that. The knowledge of this island is worth a fortune."

"And there is nothing I can say to change your mind?"

"I'm a business woman," Mrs. LaGrance stubbornly said. "I never let an opportunity pass."

"Karen!" Zachary chided her as respectfully as he could.

"Zachary!" Mrs. LaGrance echoed mockingly.

"Then you leave me no choice," Adam stated grandly before standing in order to tower over the group. He took in a deep breath, adopting a grave manor. "Tell them what you want, I don't care. The only reason you found the island was because Julianne brought you here, so none of your people will find it again. But you must go back… all of you."

"So, we can go and find Brody?" Bridie asked for clarification.

"Yes."

Bridie couldn't believe how relieved she was, but she found herself so confused. It had been so clear to her when she and Brody had decided to split up and be friends again that it was the right thing to do, but now that they had been separated, her feelings were muddled. Did she love him as her best friend, or was she fooling herself to imagine she wasn't in love with him?

"Take an hour to rest and feed," Adam advised the group. "And then we will journey to the east."

"To the forbidden zone?" Bridie asked.

"What?"

"Is it a forbidden zone?"

Adam looked a little baffled. "No."

"In the movies, there is always a place called the forbidden zone in these sorts of stories."

"The place we're going isn't forbidden," Adam logically argued.

"Okay, but I'm going to call it the forbidden zone."

"As you wish," Adam said. "When we get there, Benedict will probably not be happy to see us. He will not remember us and may consider us a threat. He has no idea we exist. All he knows are his ways and his people, and it has been that way for centuries."

"Has he never explored the island?" Condy asked.

"His people are not explorers. They aren't travellers. It's somewhat ironic that Benedict has adapted to their ways and become less prone to be adaptable. Besides that, he would not have been able to pass the barrier."

Everybody waited for an explanation.

"The barrier?" Bridie eventually asked.

"Yes. There is a line separating their half of the island from ours, and it is guarded day and night."

"Guarded by who?" Edmund asked.

Julianne decided to give this answer. "Guarded by the T-Rex."

"You have a T-Rex?"

"We've already covered this. Keep up," Bridie told Edmund. "So, how do we pass the barrier?"

"We must offer the T-Rex a sacrifice," Adam said gravely.

"Ominous."

"What kind of sacrifice?"

"Never mind that for now," Adam said dismissively. "You must rest and eat. We will reconvene in one hour."

The four immortals all stood simultaneously and retreated calmly from the humans. The remaining explorers all sat at the rainbow table for a few moments, absorbing the incredible information they had received since their arrival. One by one they left the table to retrieve their food-filled clothing.

Condy wandered over to find a place to be alone. She sat under a tree, contemplating her future. Edmund bravely wandered over and stood near her.

"Erm, Condy, can I sit with you?" he asked

Condy looked up at Edmund, and she seemed to hesitate. After a while, she patted the ground next to her. "Sure," she said.

Edmund sat down and they sat in silence for a while, eating their fruit.

"Edmund?"

"Yes?"

"I know you're… into me, and I'm really very flattered and, believe it or not, I'm tempted…" Condy said while obliterating her mango.

"But…?"

Condy smiled. "But I do have a boyfriend, and I do love him."

"He treats you like shit," Edmund said, a little too aggressively.

"No, he doesn't," she lied. "Alright, he is on the possessive side, but I happen to find that attractive. I don't understand why I find it attractive, but I've always been drawn to possessive, violent men."

"Violent?"

"I mean his temper. He's never hit me. I wouldn't put up with that."

"If he does ever hit you, then you just let me know, okay?" Edmund said with genuine guardianship.

Condy smiled into her mango. "You see, that's your nature. You're a bodyguard. You're a protector. I don't need somebody to protect me. I want somebody who isn't afraid to dominate me."

"You like to be dominated?" Edmund said with surprise.

"Do you think you could do that?" she asked him, looking into his eyes for the first time in the conversation. "Could you dominate me?"

Edmund stared back at Condy, knowing what his answer had to be. "Never," he told her.

Condy went back to eating her mango. "You see. We're not compatible."

Edmund quietly ate his blue fleshy fruit which didn't have a name. "What if we were stuck on this island?" he eventually asked.

"Hypothetically?"

"Of course."

Condy gave it some thought. "Given the competition… you'd be at the top of my list."

Edmund punched the air in victory which made Condy giggle.

"I always thought you liked Brody," Edmund suggested.

"Brody? Nah!" Condy dismissed. "He's cute, but he's too much of a wimp."

"He's a nice guy!"

"Exactly. He's a wimp," Condy laughed. "Brody's the kind of guy that would jump of a cliff in the name of love. As a friend, I adore him for that, but I'm not attracted to him because of it."

"You're kind of crazy. Do you know that?"

"Do you still dig me?"

Edmund couldn't deny it. "Yes, I do."

"I've always been independent, so the idea of needing a man to look after me kind of turns my stomach."

Edmund finished his groovy fruit, wiped his hands on the grass and got to his feet. "Well, until we get back home, I've made it my responsibility to watch out for you."

"I told you, I don't need protecting," Condy stated, yet she had gratefulness in her tone.

Edmund gave her a smile and then walked back to the food stash to get some more fruit. On his way there, he passed Zachary and Mrs. LaGrance who seemed to be having a clandestine argument.

"It should never have happened. I can't believe we had sex. I don't know what I was thinking," said Mrs. LaGrance.

"You were thinking you were going to die, and so was I. Let's just expunge it from our memories and never mention it again."

"Okay. Let's never mention it again," she agreed.

Zachary bit into his strange but tasty fruit. Mrs. LaGrance ate some berries.

"It's a shame we didn't have chance to finish before the ship capsized, though," she said contrarily.

Zachary paused in the middle of a bite. He then took his mouth away from the fruit. "I thought we weren't going to mention it again?"

"You're right. You're right."

Zachary grinded his teeth on a particularly stringy bit of fruit. Mrs. LaGrance began peeling a banana.

"We cheated," she said after a while. "We cheated on our partners and we didn't even get to finish. It seems almost sinful to betray our loved ones for something we didn't even fully enjoy."

Zachary swallowed his mouthful and heaved a sigh. "What are you talking about?"

"I'm suggesting we finish what we started. We've already been unfaithful. We might as well salvage what we can from the situation."

Zachary pondered over Mrs. LaGrance's proposal. "When?"

"We've got about half an hour."

"Okay."

Zachary and Mrs. LaGrance hurried into the woods to complete their adulterous tryst.

Twenty-one minutes later, Adam rallied up the crowd ready for their journey across the island. "Is everybody here?" he asked. The group looked around at each other, noticing two absences.

"Mrs. LaGrance and Zachary are missing," Bridie observed.

Adam closed his eyes for a moment. "I know where they are," he said after opening his eyes again.

"In the throes?"

Adam nodded and headed into the woods. His telepathic ability had told him exactly where they were and what they were up to. Adam found them humping in a small clearing surrounded by bushes. He stood behind them for a few moments, watching with bemusement and disgust.

"We are starting the journey in one minute. I must insist you re-join the party," Adam bellowed at them in a masterful tone.

Zachary and Mrs. LaGrance yelped and turned to face him as soon as he had started talking. Their expressions ranged from shocked to ashamed to embarrassed.

"And stop doing that!" Adam insisted before returning to the rest of the group.

Zachary turned to look at Mrs. LaGrance beneath him. "We've got one minute."

Mrs. LaGrance sighed. "I'm not anywhere near."

Zachary snorted. "Me neither," he said and rolled over onto his back.

Both Mrs. LaGrance and Zachary tried to catch their breath. "Maybe next time."

When they joined the camp again, the adulterous couple found everybody waiting for them. There was a strange, uncomfortable atmosphere hanging in the air, and they realised that everybody knew what they had been up to. Avoiding eye contact with each other and everybody else, Mrs. LaGrance and Zachary collected up some of the provisions for the journey and tried to blend in and become unseen.

“I want everybody to ignore the fact that these two animals spent their allocated feeding time rutting in the woods,” Adam said to the group. “Just put it out of your minds. Forget you had any idea it happened. We all need to concentrate fully on the journey ahead, and not be distracted by the lurid actions of two lustful sinners.”

“Alright, we get the point,” Zachary impatiently interrupted.

Adam laughed at Zachary’s impudence, and then began leading the journey. “Let’s go!”

The exodus of travellers followed behind. The four immortals led the group, and the humans kept a little distance. None of them was particularly keen to be too near the front having heard about the T-Rex and that there was going to have to be a sacrifice of some kind. The journey began with a certain amount of fear and excitement but very quickly became a dull chore for everyone involved. The humans had already been travelling for over a day to get to Adam’s little camp and now they were off again. The only person who still had any sense of positive anticipation was Bridie, who was thinking about only one thing – seeing Brody again.

As the journey lingered on and the humans became more restless and impatient, one of the party decided to say something about it.

“We need a break,” Mrs. LaGrance said to the immortals on behalf of everybody.

“We’re almost there,” Adam replied without altering a step or even turning around.

“Almost where?” Bridie asked.

"We're almost at the barrier," Julianne told them. She, at least, turned when she spoke to them. Julianne's time with the humans before arriving on the island had given her a modicum of familiarity with them that bordered on affection. True, Adam had stated that he loved them all, in a paternal sort of way, but it couldn't be detected on his face or in his actions.

"Does that mean…?" Condy began to ask, but her pending question was answered, before it was asked, by an enormous, rattling roar that shook the air and vibrated the ground they walked on. It was the roar of a massive creature similar to the dinosaurs in Jurassic Park. Everybody realised it had to be the call of the T-Rex. They all stopped walking, even the immortals. Zachary ran over to Adam.

"So, what's the sacrifice?" he asked. "Because, if it's a virgin, we haven't got one."

Adam looked at Zachary with a mixture of confusion and revulsion.

"Except for you immortals, obviously." Zachary carried on.

Adam opened his mouth to reply but he was interrupted by another tremendous roar that echoed across the land. The proximity of the source of the roar was clearly much closer than the previous time and everybody froze, scanning their surroundings for the owner of the cacophony. Nobody could see the alleged dinosaur.

"Where is it?" Mrs. LaGrance asked.

"It's close," Adam replied. "But it won't come out until we cross the line."

"What's the line?"

Adam took several steps forward until he reached a narrow path that ran through the grass. The path ran from left to right and went as far as they could see in both directions. The others in the group stepped forward to see what Adam was looking at.

"Prepare yourselves," Adam said and before anybody could object or have a second thought, he stepped over the line. The loudest roar the group had heard so far erupted and everybody immediately covered their ears protectively. The ground began to seriously quake with a general rumble accompanied by the rhythmic thuds of the approaching footfalls of a monstrous creature.

"Look!" cried one of the crewmen who nobody knew the name of, pointing to the west with a terrified expression.

The rest of them turned and saw the T-Rex for the first time. It was exactly as the humans had imagined. It looked just like they had all seen in the movies.

"Nobody move!" Bridie cried authoritatively. "Its vision is based on movement."

"You're basing that on Jurassic Park!" Condy accused her, keeping her eyes fixed on the huge, lumbering T-Rex.

"No, I'm basing it on the fact that I'm a palaeontologist. I'm basing it on science and research."

"What research?"

Bridie hesitated. "The works of Michael Crichton mainly," she confessed.

"You're wrong, anyway," Adam interrupted. "Its vision is based on the fact that it has a perfectly functioning pair of eyes."

The T-Rex was now standing only metres in front of them. The humans were all frozen with fear and they stared up at the dinosaur in awe and extreme trepidation. Another colossal roar came from the gaping mouth of the Tyrannosaur, and a number of the humans screamed in response. The jaws of the monster stretched impossibly wide and the emerging shriek struck terror into their hearts. Slowly, menacingly the dinosaur reached its head down to carefully examine the crowd. It sniffed and growled and made eye contact with each of the humans and the immortals.

"Shouldn't we be running away?" Zachary asked, too afraid to move.

The T-Rex gave another roar and, this time, all the humans screamed. Condy was the only one who managed to move. She hid herself behind Edmund and put her arms across his belly.

"Protect me," she whispered into his ear. Edmund smiled on the inside even though he was petrified on the outside. He took hold of Condy's arms as if to offer her comfort but, really, it was to comfort himself. After the roar died down, there was a moment of terrified silence.

"Hello," said the T-Rex.

Everybody went even quieter than they were before.

"Did the T-Rex just say hello?" Condy asked.

"Of course he did!" Adam replied. "He has manners."

"It's a T-Rex!" Bridie inserted. "Famously ill-mannered!"

"I would appreciate it," the T-Rex began, "if you would not refer to me in the third person."

Bridie looked up into the eyes of the T-Rex and felt very, very small. "I'm sorry," she apologised. "Although, I'm not entirely sure you're technically a person."

The T-Rex stood up straight and seemed to be smiling at Bridie.

"We're all just a bit surprised. We had no idea dinosaurs talked," Bridie carried on.

"Except in Jurassic Park 3, when that raptor says 'Alan'," Condy corrected, but with irony.

"That was a dream sequence."

"None of the sequels were as good as the original," the T-Rex said.

The humans were staggered. "You've seen Jurassic Park?"

"Hasn't everybody?"

"Henry," Adam then said to the T-Rex, "We are here to request safe passage to the other side of the island."

"The T-Rex is called Henry," Bridie said in a kind of trance.

"Adam, you may have access, of course," the T-Rex replied. "But you know there has to be a sacrifice."

"I understand."

The T-Rex scanned the group, looking for a candidate. None of the humans knew exactly what the sacrifice was, but they were confident it couldn't be anything good. When the T-Rex saw Condy cowering behind Edmund, he pointed at her with his little arms. "This one!" he said.

"Me?" Edmund asked.

"No, the one behind you."

Edmund turned and looked into Condy's terrified face, and then he faced the T-Rex again. "No. I have sworn to protect this woman. You may not take her!"

Everybody was, frankly, astonished – especially Condy. Edmund had been a great bodyguard and protector, but nobody could quite believe he was now squaring up to a T-Rex. Even the T-Rex seemed mildly surprised.

"This woman must make the sacrifice, or you shall not pass!"

"The Fellowship of the Ring!" Bridie said, unable to stop herself from identifying the accidental four-word movie quote.

Adam looked at Condy and Edmund. "The boarder-keeper's decision is final. If you want to cross the border, we must accept his request."

Bridie stood next to Condy who held tightly onto Edmund. "Condy, I want to see Brody again. I still love him, I think, but I won't trade your life for him."

Condy tried to smile for Bridie but she was too terrified. Bridie could see that Condy was relieved under the terror. Edmund turned to look at both of the girls. "Bridie," he said. "You're going to see Brody again." Edmund then turned once again to face the T-Rex. "Take me instead!" he insisted.

The T-Rex seemed to consider this. "No."

"Isn't this sacrifice thing up for any negotiation?" Zachary asked, wanting to help resolve the situation.

"No negotiation," the T-Rex stated damningly. "The woman must make her sacrifice, or you shall not pass!"

"Fellowship of the Ring," Bridie said again, under her breath.

"I'll do it," Condy said, almost breaking into tears.

"No, you won't!" Bridie cried.

"No, you won't!" Edmund insisted.

Bride stepped forward and spoke clearly towards Adam and Henry. "We will not sacrifice her life, or anybody's life just to be reunited with our lost friend. We shall not pass the border."

"Yes, you will!" Adam insisted. "This journey isn't only about you finding your friend, it's about all of you leaving the island together. This must happen."

Nobody had a response to this at first. "What are you gonna do about it?" Edmund asked, confrontationally.

Adam paused for a moment. "If you will not leave the island," he began grandly, "you will all have to be terminated."

"You'll kill us?" Condy screamed.

"We do not want to, but you cannot stay here. This island is not intended for your species, and you must cease to be here… one way or another."

"Well, that settles it," Condy said. "Either I sacrifice myself, or we all die. I don't really have a choice."

"There must be another way?" Edmund begged. "I will protect her until my dying breath."

The T-Rex took a step forward and gave a small growl just as a warning. "Before this gets messy, I should point out that maybe you have all misunderstood what the sacrifice is."

Everybody became attentive to Henry.

"It's my life, isn't it?" Condy said.

"No," Henry plainly stated. "You must make a sacrifice of my choosing, but the nature of the sacrifice will not be revealed to you until the relevant time."

Condy considered this with some relief. Only some. "But I won't have to die?"

"You will not."

"But I have to agree to it now, and you won't tell me what I need to sacrifice until later?"

"Correct."

Condy smiled a little at not having to give her life but was still concerned about not knowing what she was going to give up. She then looked to Edmund for support. Edmund winked at Condy and then eyed up the T-Rex. "If she is hurt in any way by this sacrifice, T-Rex, I'm coming to get you!"

"Go, Rambo!" Bridie cried, not just in aggressive support of Edmund's machismo, but also to celebrate the quote from Rambo First Blood Part 2.

"Fair enough," the T-Rex accepted with some amusement. "Condy, do you accept the terms?"

Condy blanched slightly at the sound of a T-Rex saying her name. "Yes, I agree."

"Then, you shall pass."

"Woo!" Bridie chirped.

“Thank you, Henry,” Adam said to the T-Rex as he led the crowd over the threshold, across the border and towards Benedict’s camp.

As he walked past, Edmund stared out the T-Rex.

## CHAPTER NINE
## "REUNITED"

"So, why can't Rose talk?" Brody asked Benedict.

Brody, Benedict and Rose were sitting together on some smooth stones which had been arranged near the centre of the camp.

"Her brain has no language centre," Benedict replied. "Like all her people, she has vocal cords so she can make noises to communicate, but she cannot discern language."

Rose was clinging onto Brody's arm as he and Benedict talked. Brody remarked to himself how contrary Rose was to him. He had seen her act confident and leader-like in front of her people and, also, when she had rescued him from the shipwreck, she had been a compassionate and competent nurse, but now she seemed extremely dependent on him. That he loved her, he knew for certain. Brody was self-aware enough to know that he had a tendency to over-romanticise his relationships, but this time, it was like he finally understood what it meant to be in love. It also occurred to him that it might be due to a level of chauvinism that he so quickly fell in love with a woman who couldn't answer back, but he decided to dismiss this thought as being far too cynical.

"So, if she can't discern language, does that make her…" Brody started to ask, but then hesitated. "Does it mean she's less intelligent than us?"

Benedict laughed and then shook his head. "No. That's like saying you're more stupid than a bird because you can't fly. Rose and her people are as intelligent as your kind, they just have far less ambition, and they can't talk."

"And why do they revere her?"

Benedict laughed again. "Don't you?"

Brody smiled and glanced at his new wife. She gave him her gorgeous smile. "When a girl looks at you like she looks at me, you have no choice but to worship her."

"Well, her people look up to her because she is their princess. She was chosen as their royal symbol because she is smart and caring and endlessly endearing. I don't know why she chose you, but I trust her judgement."

"Thank you," Brody said appreciatively. "So, how do you communicate with her? I realise it's some form of telepathy, but if she has no language centre, how can you talk to her in her mind?"

"With pictures," Benedict said. "I show her a series of pictures in order to convey an idea, and she creates pictures to communicate with me. All her people do it, but Rose is particularly artistic in that area."

"Have you ever tried to teach them to speak?" Brody asked.

"It's not possible," Benedict asserted. "It is simply not possible. It would be like teaching a dog to play a musical instrument. Like I said, the part of the brain that controls language isn't there. Only an idiot would think it was possible."

"So, you haven't tried it?"

Benedict paused. "Well, okay, once or twice I've given it a go, but with very little success."

"Very little success? So, you have had *some* success?"

Benedict sighed. "Some of the brighter ones are capable of a certain amount of mimicry when it comes to creating vocal sounds, but without the ability to comprehend language, they will never be able to create sentences. And besides that, even their mimicry is limited."

"Some of the brighter ones? Like Rose?"

Benedict sighed again. "Okay, fine, I'll show you."

Ben then turned to look at Rose. He put his hands gently on her shoulders and peered into her eyes. Rose returned his gaze looking a little confused. Benedict then put one of his fingers to his lips to indicate to Rose that she should try to copy him. "Brody," he said to her, slowly.

Rose turned to look at Brody. Brody gasped. "She recognised my name!"

"Not necessarily," Benedict suggested. "She might just be looking to her husband for support. Maybe she's not sure what I'm trying to do. And even if she did recognise your name, it doesn't constitute an understanding of language, it simply means that she associates you with a particular sound."

Benedict turned Rose's face to look at him again. "Brody," he repeated, more slowly this time.

Brody watched Rose carefully and he could see that she was trying very hard to copy the sound Benedict was making. As hard as she tried, no sounds came out of her mouth. Benedict decided to try a new sound.

"Ben," he said slowly. Rose did her best to copy him but the best she could manage was to make the "buh… buh" sound.

"Keep trying," Brody said excitedly.

"Ben," Benedict repeated. "Ben," he said again, extra slowly.

Rose continued to make the b sound but nothing more came out.

"Benedict," Ben then tried.

"If she can't say Ben, she's not going to master Benedict, is she?" Brody criticised.

"If I give her more to work with, there might be a part of the word that she *can* say," Benedict replied churlishly. He focussed on Rose again. "Benedict."

Rose now started making a d sound. "Duh… duh…" she uttered.

"Ben-e-Dict!" Ben said.

"Duh… duh… Dick!" Rose managed to express.

"Dick?" Brody repeated with a giggle in his voice and a smile on his face. "She said Dick!" he said, and he grabbed hold of his wife and hugged the hell out of her. He then gave her a huge kiss on the cheek.

Rose looked at Brody with a mixture of alarm and joy. She was pleased he was excited by the sound she had made. "Dick!" she said again.

"Dick!" Brody squealed.

Benedict laughed at Brody's enthusiasm, but he felt he had to temper it a little. "Okay, don't get too excited. She's just copying a sound. You have to accept that her brain isn't capable of ever grasping language."

Brody looked into Rose's eyes and brushed her hair over her ear. "I know. I just wish I could tell her I love her, and that she could understand."

"Look at her face," Benedict said. "She knows you love her."

Brody and Rose gazed at each other for a moment, and Brody realised something that, of course, he already knew, that there were many forms of communication other than language. Every time they looked at each other, they were saying 'I love you'.

"Dick!" Rose said again.

Brody laughed warmly. "Do you know what is confusing me the most?" he asked Benedict.

"What?"

"When I look at her face, I can see she's intelligent. It's in her eyes. But the fact that she can't speak makes her seem primitive. I'm having trouble reconciling those conflicting feelings."

"Maybe you're not as smart as you think," Benedict suggested, wryly.

Brody took the suggestion well. "Maybe you're right."

"Their intelligence manifests in other ways. For instance, they are all exceptionally adept at mathematics."

"Maths?" Brody said. "She's good at maths?"

Benedict smiled knowingly and then he reached behind one of the stones they were sitting on and produced a piece of slate and a stick of chalk. Brody watched as Benedict wrote something on the slate and then he showed it to Rose, passing her the chalk. Brody watched in wonder as Rose examined what Benedict had written on the slate.

"2,075 x 46," Brody read aloud. "You don't expect her to…"

Brody stopped talking as he saw Rose chalk out an answer on the slate. She wrote with dexterity and with a speed that surprised Brody. He looked at what she had written. " = 95450," he read. Brody looked up at Benedict in astonishment. "Is that right?"

"Work it out for yourself," Benedict suggested.

Brody stared at the sum for a moment and pretended to do the maths. "That's too advanced for me," he said, gazing at Rose in awe, but he couldn't help being a little cynical. "Did you set this up?" he asked Benedict. "Did you coach her to chalk out those symbols?"

"You do it, then," Benedict advised. "Give her your own sum to solve but make it one that you can work out yourself so you can be sure."

"Alright," Brody said, taking the slate and chalk. He wrote '250 x 88'. Rose took the slate from him, giving him a look that distinctly said, 'is that the best you can do?' She wrote ' = 22000' without taking her eyes off Brody. He took the slate from her but found it difficult to take his eyes away from her gaze. Rose glanced her eyes at the slate and then back at Brody as a signal for him to have a look at her answer. He did. Brody didn't know if it was right. It seemed odd to him that it was such a round number.

He began the calculation, showing his working out on the slate as he went.

"Okay, let's see. If I do 100 times 88 first, that's 880," he said as he chalked.

Rose took the chalk gently from his hand and added another zero to 880.

"Oh, of course, it's 8800, not 880. Okay, so if I double that I get… 16000… and… no, 17600, right?"

Brody wrote '88000 x 2 = 17600' and looked to Rose for confirmation. Rose smiled sweetly and nodded.

"Okay, so now I half 8800 to get 50 x 88 which is 4400, that's easy, and I add the two together, 17600 and 4400 which equals… 22000!" Brody concluded. He looked at Rose proudly. Rose looked proudly back at Brody and she clapped her hands. He kissed Rose on the forehead and laughed with fever. "She's a genius!" he exulted.

"I told you she was bright. They all are, but she's one of the smartest of them. You see, your species uses an enormous amount of brain power concentrating on lingual communication. Without that distraction, their species has developed other skills and talents."

"But how can she write numbers but not words?" Brody asked.

"Because they're numbers, not words," Benedict simply replied. "She comprehends numbers. She doesn't comprehend words."

"Maybe there is some way I can use mathematics to communicate to her," Brody conjectured. "How can I say 'I love you' in maths?"

"I have no idea," Benedict replied.

Brody had a thought, a simple but expressive thought. He picked up the slate and chalk again, and he wrote a number 1. He raised his index finger to symbolise one. "One," he said to Rose. Rose wasn't sure what he was doing, and neither was Benedict. Brody then pointed to himself. "One," he said again. He then pointed to the 1 on the slate. "One."

Rose nodded. She seemed to understand that the one he had written on the slate represented Brody.

Brody then wrote a plus sign. "Plus," he said, and then, next to the plus, he wrote another one. "One." Brody raised his index finger again. "One," he said and this time he pointed to Rose. "One," he said and then pointed at the second number 1. Next he drew an equals sign and handed the chalk to Rose to finish the sum. Rose seemed to be following him so far that the two number ones in the sum represented her and Brody. She took the chalk and effortlessly wrote a number two after the equals sign. Brody smiled, but then he rubbed out the two and, in its place, he wrote a number one. He looked into Rose's eyes to see if she understood. She seemed a little confused, so Brody iterated. "One," he said pointing to himself. "Plus," he said pointing to the plus sign on the slate. "One." He pointed to Rose. "Equals." He pointed to the equals sign, and then he took both her hands and clasped all four of their hands together to symbolise union. He raised his index finger. "One," he said. Rose's gaze shifted repeatedly from their joint fists to Brody's eyes a couple of times as she worked it out. And then, she understood. She fixed her eyes on Brody, and she smiled like it was the happiest moment of her life. A single tear escaped from her left eye and trickled down her cheek.

"That was brilliant," Benedict congratulated Brody. "You're quite clever."

"Thanks," Brody said, leaving his eyes on Rose's.

"One plus one equals one," Benedict said. "It's beautiful."

Further down the camp, a rhythmic metallic beat began to sound. It was quite a sophisticated and coordinated collection of rhythms. Benedict and Rose got immediately to their feet and turned in the direction of the sound. Brody watched them stand and then joined them. "What's going on?" he asked.

Rose took his hand without looking at him.

"That music is their way of signalling danger," Benedict revealed. "It's coming from the edge of the camp. Come on,"

Not far away from Benedict's camp, Adam's group were approaching. There were many conversations going on amongst the group establishing anticipation over where they were going and what they would find. Adam seemed to have explained everything and they had no reason not to trust him, but there is always a huge difference between being told about something and then experiencing it for yourself.

Bridie ran up to the front of the line of travellers to talk to Adam. "You know, my profession back home is palaeontology. Do you know what that is?"

Adam laughed. "Yes. You study the past."

"You could put it that way I suppose," she admitted. "Well, I'm curious about the T-Rex, about Henry. Are there more dinosaurs on this island?"

"Henry is the first dinosaur in the same way that I am the first man."

Bridie absorbed this information and made the logical assumptions. "Does that mean he's immortal?"

"Yes. He is the first and only immortal dinosaur," Adam stated.

"Have there been other dinosaurs here in the past?"

"Yes. Henry fashioned mortal versions of himself and he designed many variations as well. I'm sure you know this from your excavations."

Bridie faltered slightly at Adam's words. "So, what happened to the dinosaurs? Did you send them out into our world like you did with us?"

"Not exactly," Adam explained. "They thrived on this island for a while but there was a fundamental flaw in their genetic design."

"Which was?"

"Insatiable hunger," Adam said. "They just ate each other. They ate each other into extinction, so we took all the bones and buried them all across your world."

This time, Bridie physically stopped as she considered Adam's words. "You buried them?"

"Yes, we didn't want our island cluttered up with dinosaur bones."

Bridie was starting to think Adam was winding her up. "So, when did you do this?"

"It's hard to say. When you're immortal, you don't have a very good concept of the passage of time, but if I had to guess, I'd say it was about two thousand years."

This time, Bridie nearly fell over. "Two thousand years? Are you sure you've got that right?"

"Steve," Adam called to his partner who was several steps ahead of them. Steve dropped back to join Bridie and Adam.

"What's up?"

"How long ago, would you say, it was when we sent out the dinosaur bones for burial?"

"Oooooh," Steve replied, making sucking and clicking sounds as he considered the answer. "Two or three thousand years, I would imagine."

"That can't be right," Bridie insisted. "Are you two messing with me? Is this a joke?"

There was a pause. Bridie was expecting the two of them to start laughing, like they had done when they had bluffed about planning to kill the human race. They didn't start laughing. "We're telling the truth."

"Adam is superior to you in every way. Why would he bother to lie to you?"

Bridie shook her head. "To amuse himself, perhaps?"

"What makes you doubt us?" Steve asked her.

"Because, where I come from, we have done scientific tests and analysis and our discoveries have led us to understand that the dinosaurs lived on the Earth and died out hundreds of millions of years ago!" Bridie passionately related.

Adam and Steve both laughed at Bridie's naivete. "I think there's something wrong with your scientific tests," Adam eventually said.

"No, no, no," Bridie went on. "We know for certain that the dinosaurs were around that long ago and that they went extinct that long ago because we can measure the range of radioactivity that the fossils and rocks we discover contain. You see, radioactivity is like a clock, it has a time-stamp and we can date our discoveries pretty accurately…"

"Your science is wrong, Bridie. It is simply wrong. I don't know anything about your radioactivity, but what I do know is that we buried those bones a couple of thousand years ago. You aren't going to convince me that I'm wrong. I was there!"

Bridie followed along, lost in thought, and struggling to accept what Adam was telling her. "What about us?" Bridie eventually asked. "Humans. How long have we been around?"

Adam considered the question. "We created the first-tiers after the dinosaurs and then you guys a couple of hundred years after that."

"But that's ridiculous!" Bridie exclaimed. "Our scientists have calculated that our species has been around for a good two hundred thousand years. We can't have got it that wrong."

"Does it really matter?" Adam seemed disinterested. In fact, Bridie realised that all the immortals seemed to be generally disinterested, and particularly dispassionate.

"Yes, it really matters!" Bridie asserted. "It's the basis of all our understanding of where we came from and where we fit in the universe."

"Sorry to tell you this, Bridie, but your understanding is all wrong. You were created here, by us, less than two thousand years ago. Those are the facts."

Bridie fell behind the immortals as she considered whether or not she was willing to believe Adam's assertion. She couldn't fathom any reason for him to lie, unless he was just being cruel. Her thoughts on the subject were interrupted when the group collectively became aware of a new sound in the air. Near in the distance, a rhythmic metallic beat drifted towards them. It almost sounded like the primitive drums of a native tribe, the kind of thing you get in movies all the time, except that the rhythm was more elaborate than primitive. The travellers all stopped walking, including the immortals.

"We're here," Adam said to the group.

Continuing through the light wooded area they had come to, the group slowly came upon the source of the drum beat. Standing at the edge of what seemed like a crudely arranged village, were four naked humans using their hands to play out the beat on two large metallic instruments. Accompanying them were three dancers doing something that looked like a war dance. As soon as the musicians caught sight of Adam's party, they stopped playing and rose to their feet, backing away nervously and at ease.

"Hello there," Adam said. He was well aware that these were first-tier humans and that they weren't capable of understanding him or answering. He had spoken only to inform them of his ability to, and to establish his superiority. It was an effective strategy. The four drum beaters and three dancers turned and ran into their village, making inarticulate wailing sounds as they scarpered. Adam took hold of Sabrina's arm and whispered into her ear. Sabrina nodded understanding and made her way to the back of the group to obscure herself. Adam and his group made their way to the edge of the village and onto the outskirts of the primitive civilisation. As they progressed into the village, they saw several of the naked first-tier humans emerging from their tents and huts, looking nervous but curious. It wasn't long before they were greeted, at a distance, by Benedict accompanied by Brody and Rose.

"Brody!" Bridie cried out as soon as she saw him.

"Bridie!" he replied excitedly. Rose squeezed his hand jealously, so Brody turned and gave her a reassuring look which Rose interpreted reasonably. Brody then turned to look at Bridie again. "I thought you were all..." he said without being able to say dead.

"I thought I'd lost you," Bridie said, trying not to get too worked up about him holding hands with the pretty native girl. "Who's your friend?" she couldn't stop herself from asking.

"Er..." Brody began before he was interrupted.

"Who are you people?" Benedict asked on behalf of the village.

Adam stepped forward and held out his arms. The two groups were keeping their distance for the time being. "My name is Adam. Me and my people reside on the other side of the island!"

"The forbidden zone!" Benedict exclaimed.

"I told you there's always a forbidden zone," Bridie said excitedly. Brody smiled at Bridie's giddiness, suddenly realising how much he had missed her, even though it had only been a couple of days.

"Benedict," Adam said. Benedict visibly flinched. "You are unable to remember us."

"I have never seen you before," Benedict claimed.

Adam saw no reason to disguise the truth. "We were forced to banish you and subdue some of your memories. You were once one of us, but when we parted ways, you chose to take care of the first-tier humans. I always held respect for that."

As the immortals spoke and clumsily reacquainted, Bridie found herself slowly leaving her group and edging towards Brody, finding it hard not to take her eyes off Rose and the fact that she was holding Brody's hand. "Who's your friend, Brody?" she asked again.

At this point, Adam noticed that Bridie had separated from the group and closed in on Brody's vicinity. "Bridie, stay back until we have established grounds," Adam warned her.

"Why are you holding her hand?" Bridie asked Brody, ignoring Adam.

Everybody watched.

Brody looked nervously at Bridie and at the audience watching them. "Bridie, before I tell you about her, I need you to concur with me that you and

I broke up, amicably? We are just friends now… and I hesitate to use the word 'just' in that way as if being best friends, like we are, is in some way less than being in a relationship."

Bridie was close to them both now. Rose's grip on Brody's hand tightened as she witnessed the obvious tension between Brody and this girl.

"You're babbling, Brody, like you always do when you're nervous," Bridie said, trying to keep her manner as calm and jovial as possible, but being unable to control the fire that was burning underneath. "Yes, I concur that we broke up," she said slowly, "but then we… fumbled when the ship was sinking, and we didn't resolve what that meant."

"Bridie, honey…" Brody said to her as tenderly as he could. Everybody was captivated by the drama that was unfolding before them. Even Adam and Benedict were silently lost in the situation. "I honestly mean this when I tell you that I love you, and I will always love you…"

Rose wasn't happy about what she was hearing. She didn't understand the words, but it wasn't difficult for her to detect the emotion of what Brody was saying. Brody could sense Rose's fear and he pulled her closer to him as a reassurance that she was safe and he still belonged to her.

"You're my best friend, Bridie and I want to introduce you to Rose," Brody said, turning to look into Rose's eyes. Bridie watched in a state of near horror as she saw plain love passing between the pair. Brody turned back to look at Bridie. "She's… my wife," he revealed as sensitively as he could.

Bridie just stared at him. She just stood there and stared at him. All the other members of Adam's group had listened to the whole conversation. They just stood there and stared at Brody as well. Bridie punched him on the arm, feebly, but with weary passion. "Your wife? Excuse me, your wife? How long have you known her? A day?" Bridie said quietly but with trembling lips.

Brody knew there was trouble brewing. "About a day and a half."

Bridie punched him on the arm again, this time a little harder. Rose watched with bewildered concern. She was having trouble comprehending what this girl's relationship to Brody could be. She was a little worried that this talking girl was his wife, too, by the way she was upset. Bridie punched Brody a third time, but this time it was with both fists and on his chest. The blow sent him back a couple of steps. What was it with the women in his life that they ended up punching him? This was literally the final blow for Rose, and she launched herself protectively at Bridie, taking her to the ground and bashing her repeatedly with each fist on the head and torso. Brody, as quickly and gently as he could, grabbed hold of Rose's arms and with stern but loving persuasion, guided her to dismount Bridie and stop attacking her. Condy, always the doctor, ran over to Bridie to attend her wounds.

"I'm okay," Bridie assured her, and Condy helped her to her feet. "You punch like a girl," Bridie said to Rose, half-joking.

"She can't understand you," Brody told Bridie. "Her people have no language centre of the brain."

"She's one of the primitives!" Bridie choked. "You married a girl you can't even talk to?" Bridie went on with ridicule. "Of course you did. God forbid your wife should be able to answer back."

Brody laughed at Bridie's implication that he married a subordinate. "You've seen the way she answers back. She defends herself perfectly well."

"Have you slept with her?"

"Bridie…"

"Did you have sex with her?" she iterated sternly.

"We had to consummate the marriage," he said feeling he was making an excuse out of it. "Three times."

"I'm not upset."

"Can we talk about this later?"

The spectacle of this whole incident had fascinated everybody so much that they temporarily forgot about the more important issue at hand.

"Yes, I think the two of you should shelve this conversation for a better time," Benedict suggested. He looked across at Adam, Steve and Julianne with a glimmer of recognition. "I must admit, I have been expecting a visit from somebody for some time. I knew the T-Rex had to be guarding something in the forbidden zone. Are you here to cause trouble? Because if you are, my people and I will defend ourselves to the death."

"That won't be necessary. We have come for the boy," Adam said pointing at Brody.

Brody objected to being called a boy, he was twenty years old. He also objected to what Adam was saying. "What do you want with me?"

"We want to reunite you with your people," Adam proposed.

Brody wasn't sure what to say in response. As far as he could see, the situation ahead was surely going to become very complicated. He was glad to see everyone again, especially Bridie, but he wasn't prepared to leave Rose if anyone was going to suggest that. "Who is he?" Brody asked Bridie. A conversation continued between Benedict and Adam which only served to establish that Benedict didn't know who the strangers were and that Adam would explain shortly.

Bridie leaned in to talk to Brody. Despite the obvious tension between them, they were always going to be friends. "That's Adam. As in the first man."

"Oh," Brody said with false casualness. "He's not as tall as I expected."

Bridie frowned. "He is quite tall."

"I know, but I just thought he'd be taller," Brody continued. "Is Eve here as well?"

"No, I've a funny feeling that something got lost in translation over the years. Adam's partner is standing next to him."

"What? Julianne?" Brody abducted inaccurately.

"No, on the other side."

"That man?" Brody said, this time with genuine shock. "Are you telling me that the first couple, the two people who spawned the human race, are gay?" Brody asked with humorous bluster.

"Well, apparently they don't have a sex life, but essentially, yes. Have you guessed what Adam's partner's name is yet?"

Brody examined Bridie's face and found it to be mischievous and atheistic. "How would I guess…?" Brody stopped as the answer dawned on him and he produced the widest grin he could do. "Oh, tell me it's Steve!"

Bridie jumped in the air excitedly. "Adam and Steve! The first couple are actually Adam and Steve!"

Brody laughed triumphantly but in a whisper. "Oh my God! After all those protestors for all those years kept yelling out 'It's Adam and Eve, not Adam and Steve' and now it turns out it *is* Adam and Steve, and not Adam and Eve! That's perfect."

Rose stood dutifully next to Brody during his conversation with Bridie, feeling a bit left out while the erstwhile couple caught up. Brody suddenly realised he'd been neglecting her. He looked into her eyes and caressed her cheek sensitively with his hand. Rose smiled and they kissed.

Bridie watched, slightly enviously, but more-so gooseberry-like. "She's nice," Bridie said generously as the kiss finished.

Brody smiled at Bridie's brave attempt at being diplomatic. "I'm really in love with her, you know."

"It's such a shock, Brody," Bridie sighed.

"I know. I'm still reeling from it myself."

Bridie nodded. "I don't know what to think. I've gone numb, but I have a horrible feeling that in a couple of hours it'll sink in that you got married the day after we broke up, essentially. And you told me you weren't the marrying kind!"

"I need you to be my best friend about it and not my ex-girlfriend if that's not too unfair for me to ask of you?"

Bridie offered him a tiny smile. "It's a bit unfair, but I'll try my best."

"I feel silly telling you about it because you're a cynic like me, but when I saw her face for the first time by candle-light I was in love with her. I was instantly in love with her, I just knew it. And I could see it in her face, too. She loved me back. There was chemistry. It was magical, and the fact that we couldn't communicate, made it seem even more magical."

Bridie watched Rose's eyes following her with suspicion. Bridie still considered Rose's race to be primitive and stupid and she felt sorry for her. "She doesn't like me."

Brody shook his head. "She doesn't understand your relationship with me, that's all. I think she's afraid you're going to take me away from her."

It struck Bridie at this point that, in a way, that was exactly why they were there. "Is there any way I can make her understand that I'm not a danger to her, that I'm not a rival?"

Brody thought he had the solution. "Yes, actually. It might seem a little odd or uncomfortable, but in her culture, they express friendship with a kiss on the nose."

Bridie smiled nervously. "You want me to kiss her on the nose? She just beat the hell out of me," she laughed.

"Trust me, she won't be suspicious of you after that," Brody suggested. He could see Bridie was still dubious. "Do it for me?" he said questioningly.

Bridie's eyes flitted between Brody's and Rose's for a few moments as she considered Brody's request. "Alright, but you owe me!" she insisted.

"Granted."

Bridie looked at Rose and smiled. Rose didn't smile back, not because she was hateful or grudging, but simply because she was protecting her heart. Bridie took a couple of deep breaths, tried to give Rose a reassuring look and then she leaned in and gently gave her a peck on the nose. As she leaned back from the little kiss, she half expected Rose to attack her again. Contrarily, Rose flashed an appreciative smile, bit her bottom lip endearingly and then quickly kissed Bridie on the nose in return. The message had been conveyed and Rose clung onto her husband, clearly happy and reassured.

"I can't believe it worked," Bridie said.

"She's extremely trusting. Astoundingly so, actually. Oh, and did I mention she's a princess?"

Bridie laughed at Brody's pride. "Wow! A princess, so that makes you a prince!"

Brody gasped. He couldn't believe that hadn't occurred to him until now. "Prince Brody!" he exulted.

"Don't hate me for asking, but how smart is she? I figured this first-tier race were dumb primitives, but it's clear from her eyes that she's intelligent."

Brody nodded. "She's a genius. The only reason they can't talk is that they don't have a speech centre of the brain, but they all have mad maths skills."

"Compensatory abilities," Bridie labelled.

"Exactly, and Benedict says Rose is one of their brightest. My new wife is a primitive genius!"

"New wife," Bridie repeated risibly, still not quite believing it. "How did you get married so fast?"

"To them, a single kiss on the lips is both a proposal and acceptance of marriage. To be honest, the first time I kissed her I thought it was just a kiss. Later, when Benedict told me it was how these people got married, I was stunned, and Rose knew it. When she realised that I hadn't meant to propose to her, I watched her face change and I saw her heart break and I realised that her heart belonged to me now and I had to protect it. And my heart belongs to her, and I know she will protect it. I understand how it works now. Romantic love isn't about just giving your heart to someone and hoping for the best, it's about knowing that the one person who can break your heart is the same person that you must trust to protect it."

"I think that was the most beautiful thing you've ever said," Bridie gushed. "But then, most of the things you say are shit-water, so it's not a massive achievement."

Brody laughed, and so did Rose. She didn't understand the words being said, but she was discerning enough to understand that Bridie was important to Brody and that she had accepted Rose as his wife.

The private discussion between the threesome was interrupted by the raised voice of Adam, and they realised they hadn't been paying any attention to the conversation between Benedict and Adam.

"Your name is Benedict and you are my creation!" Adam bellowed. "You will obey me or there will be consequences!" Adam was overpowering and over-dramatic.

Bridie leaned in to whisper to Brody. "Adam seems to have a people management problem."

Benedict's face was quivering with stifled rage at Adam's arrogance. Benedict still had no memory of Adam or his people and he wasn't sure what the best course of action was. The only thing he knew was that he had to protect his people. "I think you should either turn around and go back to where you came from, and take your people with you, or you should calm down, accept our hospitality and we can all talk about this rationally and as a group," Benedict soberly proposed.

Adam's fury was written all over his face, and yet he seemed to be considering Benedict's words. "I accept your suggestion," he said.

"Which one?" Benedict asked. "Going back to where you came from or talking rationally as a group?"

"Talking rationally as a group," Adam confirmed.

# CHAPTER TEN
# "TALKING RATIONALLY AS A GROUP"

Adam and Benedict's groups congregated in the centre of the first-tiers' village. Benedict's group consisted of Brody, Rose and about one hundred other muties as Benedict affectionately called them. The conversation covered a lot of ground, from Adam's decision to seek out Brody, to his rationale for insisting that the new humans must leave the island. Benedict was reluctant to insist on anything when it came to the humans except that they should have their free will and be allowed to make their own decisions. Adam disagreed. He considered that the immortals were superior and therefor, wiser and it was up to them to make the best decisions for everybody.

About an hour into the conversation, Brody had a statement to make. "If I agree to leave the island with my people, then I am taking Rose with me."

Neither Adam nor Benedict responded at first. Brody deemed from this that neither of them agreed.

"Otherwise I'm not leaving," Brody added.

"Unacceptable," Adam simply said. "She is a different species, and if your people in the outside world discover that, it will dramatically upset your society on religious and scientific grounds. We can't be responsible for that kind of change"

"We won't tell them," Brody naively suggested.

"Rose has a different anatomy to yours. Essentially all the parts are the same, but they are arranged in different places. If she visits one doctor, she will be discovered."

"Then we'll keep her away from doctors."

"Are you telling me that if the woman you love gets sick, you'll still respect my wishes?" Adam smartly asked.

If Brody had learned anything in the last hour, it was that Adam didn't respect the opinions of anybody mortal. Brody turned to the immortal who seemed the most human. "Benedict?"

Benedict shook his head before he spoke. "If you ask Rose to go with you, I am certain she will do whatever it takes to be with you, but you would be taking her away from her people, from her family, and plunging her into an alien society she doesn't understand. Please remember, her kind are happy because they find contentment in nature and music and dance and mathematics and social interaction. They have no capacity for selfishness or personal achievement. They are each a member of the group and they share collective peace and wellbeing. She would never *ever* understand your greedy, selfish, dog-eat-dog, technological world."

Brody knew from what little he had seen of Rose's people and his close observations of Rose herself, that Benedict was right. He couldn't, with good conscience, take her away from her people. "Then, I'm staying."

"Impossible!" Adam hollered.

"Brody, you have to come with us," Bridie pleaded. "Adam told us that if we don't all leave, he will terminate us."

"He's bluffing," Benedict laughed.

"I don't bluff. It's a pointless tactic."

"Brody," Bridie said, "What about me? If you stay here with Rose, you'll never see me again. Doesn't that effect you at all?"

Brody glared at Bridie with slightly moistened eyes. "Don't you see?" he said softly. "You're the reason this decision is so hard. You are the only reason I have for going home, but I have to be with Rose. She's my wife. I know you, Bridie, you won't get in the way of a commitment like that."

Bridie smiled a couple of tears. "Damn, you know me too well."

At this point, Benedict stood up. "Then I suggest a compromise. Brody stays with us. He is welcome in our community, and the rest of the second-tier humans will all willingly leave, as you command, Adam."

Everybody looked at Adam, falteringly confident that he would agree. "No," he said with an air of finality. "They *all* must go."

"Then we have a stalemate!" Benedict replied. "I am prepared to defend Brody's right to his decision, by whatever it takes."

"That's a mistake," Adam informed him.

"Take your people and leave. You are no longer welcome here," Benedict demanded.

Adam arose from the stone he was sitting on and eyed Benedict for signs of insecurity. He could only see stubborn determination in Benedict's expression. "Sabrina!"

Benedict flinched at the sound of Adam screaming Sabrina's name. The word flicked on a switch inside him which had a resonance of something familiar, but he couldn't quite access it.

"Yes, Adam?" Sabrina said after emerging unseen from some tall bushes nearby. She had been hiding there the whole time at Adam's request.

Everybody turned to see Sabrina by the bushes. When Benedict saw her for the first time, an explosion went off in his chest, his stomach did the fandango and his loins suddenly remembered what they were really for. Benedict stared at Sabrina as if he was seeing the most beautiful sunset for the first time. Her cascading red hair beautifully complemented her pink naked skin. Her curves were tight and balanced and mathematically perfect. Her face was unbelievable – sublime features topped off with an adorable sprinkling of freckles. As soon as he saw her, Benedict remembered everything he had know about her and, consequently, all his supressed memories came flooding back. Benedict remembered all the events of his banishment and of his slightly embarrassing obsession with Sabrina. Of course, the obsession returned with all its glory, and Benedict couldn't take his eyes off the auburn stunner.

"Sabrina," he said in a whimsical voice.

Sabrina took a few sultry steps towards the group. "Hello, Ben," she said. Despite all the problems she had been through with Benedict, she discovered to her surprise that she was actually pleased to see him, and that she had missed him. This was especially surprising to Sabrina because immortals weren't supposed to be able to miss people.

"How have you been?" he asked.

"Same as always."

"You look as beautiful as you ever have."

"That's because I am," she replied, slightly facetiously. "When you don't age, your looks don't change."

Benedict smiled. It was a fairly old immortals joke, but when you aren't affected by the passage of time, nothing ever gets old, not even jokes.

"You remember me, then?" Sabrina asked coquettishly.

"How could I forget?"

"Well, you did forget…" Sabrina pointed out.

"No, I didn't forget about you, the memory of you was taken from me," he said, looking accusingly at Adam. "But now I remember everything."

"Yes," Adam interjected. "When we suppressed your mind, we made the sight of Sabrina a trigger for your memories."

Benedict continued to stare at Sabrina for a while, in a daydream. Then he snapped out of it just enough to return his mind to the issue. "This doesn't change anything," he told Adam. "Giving me back my memories doesn't change who I am or what my priorities are."

"Are you sure about that?" Adam asked confidently.

Benedict hesitated. "Yes," he said uncertainly.

"Do you know that when we decided to banish you, Sabrina voted against us?"

Benedict looked across at Sabrina again. She looked away bashfully.

"No, I didn't know that," Benedict said.

"I always thought she had a secret desire when it came to you. I suspect she has been weakened by the temptation of sexuality unlike Julianne, Steve and myself."

Benedict focussed his eyes on Sabrina, attempting to see any glimmer on her face that she recognised Adam's accusation. Sabrina gave nothing away.

"Maybe you gave up on her too easily," Adam suggested.

"What?"

"If you had tried a little harder, you might have been able to win her over."

"Tried a little harder?" Benedict screamed. "I gave her everything I had. I was her perennial slave! I attended to everything she asked for, and more. I bathed her, I washed her hair, I decorated and maintained her living area. I danced for her. I wrote poetry. I sang songs. I made a fool of myself around her."

"It was very funny," Steve glibly remarked.

"Seriously, Adam, what more could I have done to court her?"

Adam gave it some thought. "You could have brought her flowers."

"Are you joking?"

Sabrina stepped forward. "I like flowers," she said.

Benedict's mouth was agape. "Then I will grow you a garden full of your favourite flowers."

"You would do that for me?" Sabrina asked slightly coyly.

"I would die for you if I wasn't immortal."

Sabrina discovered that the animal desires that she shared with Benedict which Adam had suspected she always had were galloping to the surface. But it was all too overwhelming for her to deal with and she uncharacteristically fainted.

"Sabrina!" Benedict yelled as her ran to her. He dove to be by her side and lifted up her head gently. Adam joined him followed by Condy. "What's wrong with her?" Benedict asked Adam.

Adam shrugged and looked confused. Condy put her hand on Sabrina's head and felt for a pulse. "Well, I don't know anything about her physiology, but I would say she fainted."

"Immortals don't faint," Adam insisted.

"Maybe they do if they are overcome by animal emotions. I think seeing you again, Benedict, was too much for her!" Condy surmised.

Neither Adam nor Benedict contradicted Condy's diagnosis. "Can you make her conscious again?" Adam asked.

"I'm not sure," she admitted. "I could do with a pair of Brody's socks right now."

"Hey!" Brody cried with semi-amused offense.

"Do you have anything here that smells really bad?" Condy asked.

"Erm…"

"Let me try something," Benedict said, and he leaned in close to Sabrina's ear. "SABRINA!" he yelled.

Sabrina's eyes opened and she sat up fast and rigid. "What happened to me?"

"We think you fainted," Condy told her.

"Fainted? Wow! I didn't know I could do that," Sabrina said with amazement in her tone. "It was like I was dead and then I came back to life."

"You just fell over," Adam told her.

"And then Benedict ran over here faster than anyone else even reacted," Condy said with a smile on her lips.

Sabrina looked up at Benedict. "You got to me first?" she asked.

Benedict nodded. "You scared me," he said.

Sabrina put her hand on Benedict's cheek, but her smile drained away slightly. "I don't understand what I'm feeling," she said, and she stood up, backing away from Benedict and the others. "For years you pandered to me, giving me everything I wanted, and I let you do it because it made me happy and I thought it made you happy too."

"It did."

"But today, I feel different. Today I feel like… like I want to pander to you, Benedict."

Benedict almost cried.

Sabrina turned to look at Adam. "How can this be, Adam? Immortals don't change. We don't exist in time. How can I feel differently today than I did on a previous day?"

Adam sighed. "When Steve and I created you, all three of you, we made you physically immortal, but we experimented with your emotions. Your feelings change with time even though your physical process doesn't. You're only noticing it now because it has taken a while for those emotions to develop and because your environment has drastically changed."

"Okay," Sabrina said.

"It happened a lot faster with Benedict, which is why we had problems with him," Steve added. "It was clear to us that he had fallen in love with you which destroyed his objectivity."

"And what about me?" Julianne asked. "I haven't experienced any emotional changes."

"Yes, you have," Adam corrected. "When you came back to us, you hugged me."

Julianne considered this. "Hmm. I did, didn't I?"

"But you were the one we experimented with the least. Your emotions are only slightly tweaked, so it shouldn't have as dramatic effect on you as it has on Benedict and Sabrina."

"Does that mean I can fall in love?" Sabrina asked excitedly.

Adam laughed, as if falling in love was something silly to him, which it was. "Well, Benedict did."

Sabrina looked at Benedict and gave him a hopeful smile. Benedict looked into Sabrina's eyes and he realised his priorities were changing. "I'll give you Brody if I can have Sabrina," he said coldly to Adam.

"No!" Brody objected.

"Sabrina isn't mine to give you, Benedict," Adam told him. "She has to make that decision for herself. But it is in everyone's interest for Brody to join his friends and leave this island."

"I'm staying with Rose, or she's coming with me," Brody declared again.

"Brody, do this for the rest of us," Bridie pleaded. "Do the right thing. Come back with us. Rose will be fine. Maybe you can skype her or something."

Brody didn't particularly appreciate Bridie's joke, but he knew she had done it in an attempt to ease things for him. "Why is everybody trying to persuade me to go? Why isn't anybody trying to persuade Adam to let me stay?"

Everybody looked at Adam briefly, and then Bridie gave Brody his answer. "Because you are the only one who wants you to stay."

"And Rose. She wants me to stay, too."

"Well, obviously."

Adam had a short wander around as he contemplated everything that was going on. "It seems we have a stalemate. Brody can't stay on the island and Rose can't leave. My problem is that I've seen what men in love are capable of, and I can see it in Brody's eyes. It seems I must make a compromise. Brody would sooner die than give up Rose. The question I have for him is this…" Adam walked over to Brody and put his hands on the young man's shoulders. "Brody, would you be prepared to kill for her?"

"What?"

"Dying for what you love is easy," Adam claimed. "But killing for it takes a much stronger stomach. Could you do it, Brody? Could you kill someone to be with Rose?"

Brody was understandably, extremely hesitant. He couldn't bear the thought of losing Rose, but to kill for her? He didn't think he could do it, and he didn't think Rose would want him to do it. "Who would I have to kill?" he asked meekly.

"That decision has already been made," Adam said. "When we passed the barrier to visit this side of the island, the T-Rex demanded a sacrifice from one of your friends, a sacrifice which would be paid later. That sacrifice is due now."

Adam and the others who had crossed the barrier with him turned to look at Condy. She was still sitting on the ground after attending to Sabrina's faint. Condy didn't know what to say.

"Condy?" Brody cried. "You want me to kill Condy? I can't do that."

"But the T-Rex said that I wouldn't be harmed when I gave my sacrifice."

"That's true," Adam agreed.

"The T-Rex said that?" Brody said with daydream incredulity.

"Yes," Bridie confirmed. "They have a talking T-Rex."

"Of course they do."

"Condy is correct that Henry promised she wouldn't be harmed," Adam said.

"Who's Henry?" Brody asked.

"The T-Rex," Bridie told him. "His name is Henry."

Brody stared into space. "Of course it is."

Adam continued his explanation. "Condy isn't the sacrifice. She has to make a sacrifice and live with it – that's the condition. The one she has to sacrifice is the man she's falling in love with."

"No!" Condy cried out. "And anyway, who says I'm falling in love with Edmund?"

Adam laughed. "But you knew who I was talking about."

Condy looked across at Edmund who was well within earshot. Edmund's grin went from ear to ear. "What are you smiling at?" she asked him.

"You're falling in love with me."

"Shut up!" she demanded. "Didn't you hear the bit about me having to sacrifice you. He's going to make Brody kill you so that he can stay on this island with his new mutie wife."

"Hey!" Brody objected.

"I'm not afraid to die," Edmund said magnificently.

"You should be," Condy demanded.

"You can't do the job that I do without being willing to make the ultimate sacrifice."

"Stop it. You're not at work, now."

"I'm not afraid to die… for you," Edmund gushed with sickening romanticism.

Condy's galloping feelings for Edmund suddenly intensified. "I don't want you to die."

Edmund took a step towards Condy. "If my death means that you get safely off this island and back home, then it's my honour." He took another step towards her.

"Do you know why there are so few heroes in the world?"

"Why?" Edmund asked, taking another step closer to Condy. They were only a few feet apart now.

"Because they always do the noble thing and sacrifice themselves. It's backwards, it's anti-evolutionary. Good men like you need to stick around so you can have hero kids."

Edmund took the final step towards her and they stood toe to toe. "You want me to have kids?" he asked her, cheekily.

Condy couldn't stop herself from smiling. "Yes. I do."

"And what better mother could my kids have, than another hero… like a doctor."

Condy took hold of Edmund's hand and began tickling his palm with her thumb. "I'm a doctor," she said playfully.

Everybody was watching and enjoying the flirtation between Condy and Edmund, but to Condy and Edmund, nobody else was even there. Edmund decided the time was just right and he leaned in for the kiss. Everybody watching instinctively leaned in with him. Rose squeezed Brody's hand and smiled at him to show she understood what was going on between Condy and Edmund, even though she was completely oblivious to the discussion about whether or not Brody was going to stay on the island with her. Before their lips met, Condy pushed Edmund away and everyone made an 'awww' sound in disappointment.

"Sorry," Edmund apologised in confusion. "I thought you wanted me to."

"I do want you to," she replied, slightly angrily. "I want you to live. You can kiss me when you agree to live."

Edmund looked at her sadly. "Condy, it's my duty."

"Do you care about me?"

"Yes."

"Do you want me?"

"Yes."

Condy's lip was quivering with rage. "Is your duty more important than me?"

Edmund hesitated, but he had to be true. "Yes," he replied.

"I love you, what do you think of that?" she screamed at him furiously.

"Since when?" he asked with dubious delight.

"Since now. Since just now. It just happened now," Condy flustered. "I'm in love with you as of right now."

Edmund's head was swimming. "What about your boyfriend?"

"He's my ex."

"Since when?"

"Since now. Since just now. It just happened now."

"I have to do this, Condy."

"No, you don't."

"I do."

"You love me too, don't you?" she blurted, still quivering with anger. "You're in love with me too, aren't you?"

Edmund faltered. "No," he lied.

"What do you mean, no?"

"I mean…"

"Don't lie to me. If you loved me, you wouldn't lie to me!" she shouted at him contradictorily.

"I can't say it just because you ask me to," he complained. "I can only tell you I love you if you let me say it when I mean it and not because you've asked me to say it."

"Okay, fine. Don't say it. I don't want to know," she said conspiratorially.

"You really don't want to know?"

Condy put her face right up against his. "I don't want to hear it!" she insisted.

"I love you," he said.

"I knew it!"

"I'm in love with you," he clarified.

"Then don't die!" she insisted, and then she punched him in the face. "Don't die!" she iterated.

Brody shook his head. "Ed, it doesn't make any difference. I couldn't kill anybody anyway. I won't do that, not even for Rose."

Edmund glared at Brody for a moment and then he turned to face Adam. "Does he have to kill me, or do I just have to die?" he asked.

Adam smiled. "You are the sacrifice, Edmund. It doesn't matter how you die, it just matters that you do."

"So, I could do it myself?"

"That would be sufficient."

Edmund let go of Condy and ran to a nearby area of the camp where the natives kept a stash of crudely made cutlery and cooking utensils. Edmund picked out a blade from the collection and placed it on his throat.

"Don't you dare!" Condy screamed while she chased after him. As Edmund placed the blade to his throat, Condy launched herself at him and brought him down onto his back, being careful to thrust the blade away from Edmund's throat. She sat on his stomach to hold him down and held his arms down with her hands.

"Let me do it!" he begged. "It's the right thing to do. It's the only way to save you all."

"No, it isn't!" she screamed. "All you are doing is giving your life so Brody can stay with his new girlfriend."

"They need each other!" he asserted.

"And I need you!" Condy blasted. "I need you because without you, I'm going to go back to England, get back together with my sleazy, two-timing waste-of-space boyfriend and be unhappy for the rest of my life."

"Don't do that," Edmund pleaded. "You can do better."

"But I won't," she said. "I'm too weak to try. You're right, I can do better than him, but I can't do better than you."

Edmund didn't have anything to say to this. She was winning him over, and she completed her victory by leaning down and giving him the most flaming kiss he had ever been given. Edmund was enslaved – willingly and completely enslaved and he gave up his noble aspirations.

Adam coughed to draw everybody's attention. "So, does this mean you are going to leave with your friends?" he asked Brody.

Brody turned and looked at his wife. Rose knew that something serious was going on but she hadn't fully fathomed the truth. All she knew for certain was that some new people had arrived on their island and now there was commotion, and she assumed they wouldn't all be staying. She assumed that once the commotion was over, they would go back to where they had come from. Naively, she hadn't entertained the idea that Brody might be leaving with them. Her confidence in their relationship had blinded her to the possibility that he could ever leave her. Nevertheless, Rose wanted to know what was going on. She strode over to Benedict and put his hands on her forehead as a request for him to relay to her what was going on. Benedict looked at Brody for his permission.

"Tell her the truth," Brody said. "Make sure she understands that I don't want to leave her, but I have to."

Benedict gave his focus to Rose and he stared intensely into her eyes. As he told her the situation in pictures, she became agitated and upset. Brody took hold of her hand to offer his comfort. She held on tightly and crushed his fingers. Contrary to Brody's request, Benedict omitted the part about Brody leaving her. He knew that if Rose found out now that she was going to lose Brody, she would be outraged and unmanageable. He made the dubious decision not to tell her but to pretend to Brody that he had. As Benedict reached the end of his pictorial explanation, Rose turned to look at Brody. She looked sadly into his eyes for a moment and then she pulled him to her chest and hugged him. During the hug, Brody looked to Benedict.

"She understands?" Brody asked.

"She's sophisticated and reasonable," Benedict replied. "I made her understand that you can't stay here, and she can't go with you. I made her understand that you were doing this to save your friends and that she should be very proud of you."

"Did you tell her I love her?"

"She already knows that," Benedict said. "And she wants to give you a goodbye present."

Rose pulled back from the hug and took hold of Brody's hand.

"What kind of present?" he asked.

Rose led Brody by the hand to one of the village stone huts.

"Oh, I see," Brody said as they disappeared inside.

Benedict stared after them as he imagined what was going on inside the hut. So did everybody else. Only Adam, Steve and Julianne were unaffected by the prurient nature of Brody and Rose's assumed activity. Benedict was overcome with a sensation he had neglected for too long and strode determinedly over to Sabrina. Sabrina watched him approach and did nothing to resist his dedication to the course he was bent on. When he arrived in her presence, Benedict stared into Sabrina's literally perfect eyes.

"I want you," he said.

"I know you do," she replied.

"It's your decision."

"I know it is."

Benedict was running out of things to say. He was trying to keep his conversation simple and not be too overtly obvious about what he wanted from her, but he was finding it hard.

"So, sex?" she asked. "I'm assuming you want to do sex with me. I don't know how to do it, though."

Benedict laughed. “Maybe we can explore it together?”

“Do you know how it works?” she asked. From any other woman, this would be a damning roast, but from Sabrina, it was an honest enquiry.

“I understand the mechanics of it, and I have occasionally seen the muties doing it,” Benedict explained. “They seem to enjoy it very much.”

“Why did those two go into the hut to do it just now? Why don’t they do it out in the open?”

“People prefer to do it in private. It’s an intimate moment between two people and shouldn’t be shared with anybody else.”

Sabrina thought it over for a few moments. She looked over at Adam for advice or permission.

“It’s your decision, Sabrina. You can return to ‘the forbidden zone’ with me, Steve and Julianne, or you can stay here with Benedict.”

“And what about sex?” she asked him openly. “Can it happen between immortals?”

“You clearly have an urge to try it,” Adam observed. “Like I stated before, you and Benedict are more human than we are, so you are susceptible to human urges.”

“What about letting Ben come home with us?” she asked.

Adam looked over at Benedict with an avuncular warmth. “I think he’s learned his lesson. He may return with us if he wishes. But, the first-tier humans must remain here. It is their home now.”

Sabrina looked across at Benedict to see if he would agree to come back with them. Benedict shook his head apologetically. “I can’t leave my people,” he told her. "Not even for you," he continued with some regret.

All around the village, the first-tier humans smiled and felt comforted at Benedict's loyalty. They couldn't understand what the immortals were saying to each other, of course, but Benedict had been sending them a group telepathic flick-book conveying the basic gist of the conversation.

Sabrina thought it over some more. "Alright, Ben. I will let you do sex with me now," she said as plainly as if she was suggesting they go for a walk.

Benedict's eyes nearly popped out of their sockets and his knees suddenly felt absurdly weak. "Okay," he meekly squeaked.

"And afterwards," Sabrina continued, "I will decide whether or not I'm going to stay here with you, but I must let you know that my preference is currently to go back to my home with Adam and Steve and Julianne."

"I understand," Benedict said but he was finding it hard to concentrate on anything since the moment Sabrina had said she was going to 'do' sex with him. There was a slightly awkward pause for a moment, and then Sabrina took the initiative and strode over to Benedict, taking hold of his hand and leading him to one of the huts, closing the primitive but effective door behind them for privacy.

After this, there was a moment's silence until, out of the blue, a collection of the first-tier humans picked up some of their odd-looking musical instruments and began to play a loud, ethnic, rhythmic jazz piece. Most of the other muties began to dance. Nobody was sure why they were suddenly, spontaneously dancing this way. It could have been anything from celebration to simply passing the time, but they seemed to be enjoying themselves. It did seem more recreational than ritualistic.

Mrs. LaGrance sidled over to Zachary and gave him a dirty smile. "Third time lucky?" she asked.

Zachary laughed in a warm familiar way, nodding acquiescence, and the pair ran and ducked into another one of the huts. Everybody watched as they did this, laughing and gossiping about it. Adam shook his head with amused disapproval at the animalistic conduct of the humans. "Anybody else?" he asked the crowd.

The second-tier humans all nervously looked around at each other. Edmund made a deliberate effort not to look at Condy because he was afraid if he did, she would avoid him and he would be gutted. He also didn't want her to think that was all he wanted from her, so he was trying to convey respect by avoiding eye-contact. He was avoiding her so successfully that he didn't see her approaching him, even though everybody else did. As Condy approached him, she looked across at Bridie for advice. Bridie smiled and gave her the thumbs up. Bridie and Condy both knew that she was technically being unfaithful to her boyfriend back home, but they also both knew that her boyfriend was a piece of shit who she needed to scratch out of her life, and that Edmund was a considerably better choice. Condy took hold of Edmund's hand and stared into his avoiding eyes. Edmund was too nervous to look at her at first, but eventually he returned her gaze. Her eyes told him what she was thinking, and Edmund couldn't have been happier.

"Are you sure?" he asked.

Condy didn't reply, she simply led him to one of the huts and they settled inside, closing the door behind them.

Bridie couldn't help but feel left out. She looked around at the remaining candidates among her peers, and quickly realised she wasn't getting laid that day. There were a number of cute young men among the muties, but Bridie had come to understand from what Brody had told her, that they regarded sex as being symbolic of marriage and didn't in any way consider it casually. She decided instead to join the natives in their dance fever.

Adam, Steve and Julianne decided to sit out the party on some large stones on the outside of the camp. Almost everybody else joined in the dancing with a few exceptions from the crew who stood shyly around the edge too timid to let themselves go.

After about half an hour, Brody and Rose re-emerged from their hut, looking happy and in love. Bridie saw the look on Rose's face, and it seemed to her that the girl was a little too happy for someone who had recently found out her husband was leaving forever. For the moment, she wondered how much Benedict had actually told Rose and it occurred to her that maybe Rose didn't know Brody was leaving. While Bridie considered approaching Brody with her suspicions, she was distracted by the sight of Sabrina emerging from the hut she had been sharing with Benedict. Sabrina was kind of staggering as she walked and she had a lost, daydream look about her.

As soon as Adam saw her, he stood up and walked in her direction. As Adam approached, Benedict emerged from the hut looking like he'd had sex for the first time, which, of course, he had.

Adam stopped walking when he saw the look on Sabrina's face. Sabrina seemed to recover slightly from the trance she was in, and she looked up at Adam.

"I'm staying!" she said insistently, and then she let out the joyous cry of someone who had just found out what it was like to live life. "I'm staying here with Benedict. I'm sorry, Adam."

"My child," he said with genuine affection. "You know where we are when you change your mind."

Sabrina looked puzzled. "When I change my mind?"

"All creatures of time change their mind. It's inevitable."

Sabrina smiled at Adam and then stepped away from him to return to Benedict. It was at this point that Zachary and Mrs. LaGrance emerged from their hut. They were immediately hit with a serious bout of self-consciousness as they realised all eyes were upon them. Even the dancers and musicians had stopped their activities to stare at the couple. Neither Zachary nor Mrs. LaGrance could understand why they were being stared at, but it had the effect of making them both extremely guilt-ridden about their adulterous tryst. Even the muties had been made aware of their infidelity by means of Benedict's telepathic picture painting, and unfaithfulness was something that simply didn't happen in their culture.

The muties didn't suffer from ambition and because of that, they weren't always seeking out what they didn't have, nor were they jealously pursuing other people's possessions. This simple trait made them all devout to each other and magnanimously monogamous.

Bridie approached Zachary and Mrs. LaGrance, more amused than disapproving. "So, what have you two been up to?" she asked with deliberate innocence.

Mrs. LaGrance gave a creepy, wicked smile and then she looked around the camp to find Julianne. "Julianne," she yelled to her. "What did you say the name of this island was?"

"It's ancient name is Mesaglenedendeltor," Julianne revealed.

"Well, what happens in Mesaglenedendeltor, stays in Mesaglenedendeltor," she said to Bridie mysteriously.

Bridie and several of the other second-tier humans tittered at her response.

And finally, Condy and Edmund emerged from their hut of titillation. Like all the other hut-emerging couples before them, they both seemed extremely happy with themselves and pleased with their choice. Edmund looked particularly satisfied. Holding hands, they re-joined their group. An idle, gossipy chatter emerged from the speaking members of the company. Bridie did a little more sidling, this time, in Condy's direction.

Bridie leaned in and whispered to her. "How was he?" she asked naughtily.

Condy smiled as if she wasn't going to reply. "He took care of me," she simply said.

Bridie was slightly ashamed of herself for being surprised but somehow Edmund didn't strike her as being a typical lothario in the sack. "Really?" she replied bluntly.

Still whispering, Condy explained it to Bridie. "Let's just say, as a trained bodyguard, his hands are deadly weapons!"

Bridie leaned back in amazement and couldn't help looking at Edmund in a new light. Edmund hadn't been privy to their hushed discussion and so he was oblivious to Condy's words.

"Oh my god!" Bridie silently exclaimed. "Good for you, girl," she congratulated her friend.

"Very good," Adam then cried out as a general way of taking control of the situation. "You've had your fun, but now, I'm afraid, it's time for our visitors to depart. All of them."

Brody looked into Rose's beautiful eyes and couldn't quite believe he was going to have to say goodbye to her. Rose could see that something was wrong with Brody, and her eyes pleaded with him to explain. Brody watched Rose with confusion. He couldn't understand what her expression was saying to him. It didn't occur to him at that time that Benedict hadn't told her that Brody was leaving. Instead, Brody thought that perhaps their bond wasn't as strong as he'd thought and there was still some distance between them, judging by how he couldn't read her right now. He kissed her on the nose as assurance that things were going to be okay, but inside he wanted to cry his heart out.

“We will take a trip to the nearest beach where I have a gift waiting for you all,” Adam went on. “Prepare whatever provisions you need for the journey and let us depart.”

## CHAPTER ELEVEN
## "DEPARTURE"

The journey to the beach took roughly a day. They were heading to the same beach where Brody and Rose had first met only days before. Brody was holding tightly onto his bride as they trekked across the island, sinking more and more desperately upset as each hour passed, knowing that when they reached the beach, he would have to leave her. Rose, on the other hand, seemed to be coping with it very well and it was this realisation that caused him to first suspect that Benedict hadn't been entirely truthful with her. Brody was anxious to confront Benedict with this accusation, but he was equally hesitant because he was foolishly putting off realising his suspicions. Most of the muties had stayed behind at their camp. Only Rose from the first-tiers was with the trekkers.

As they arrived on the beach, Brody had become certain that Rose didn't have any idea that this was going to be goodbye for them. Adam, who was leading the group, came to a stop in the middle of the beach, took in his surroundings, and turned to face everybody. Despite the fact that it was a glorious day, the perennial fog that surrounded the island was still present making it hard to see the ocean far beyond the shore.

"As I mentioned before we started this journey, I have a gift for the departing humans," Adam said, and he turned once again to face the sea. And he just stood there. Everybody started looking towards each other as if to say, 'what the hell is he doing?'

Eventually, they realised he was looking way into the fog bank, and that something was emerging slowly from it. As everybody made this realisation, they all squinted their eyes to try and discern what was emerging from the water. They all very soon realised it was a vessel, and shortly after that they realised it was the ship they had come to the island on. It was the ship that had wrecked and sunk to the bottom of the ocean casting them adrift and nearly killing them all.

"That's my ship!" the captain exclaimed.

"But it sank," another crew member stated.

Brody looked over at Adam. "You brought it back," he said. "You rebuilt it."

Adam turned again to look at the group. "Yes, you need a way to leave the island. What better way than by the means you arrived?"

"How did you rebuild it?" Bridie asked. "I mean, you didn't take a hammer and nails to the wrecked remains."

"Telekinesis," Adam revealed.

"Okay."

"Can you bring back people, too?" Condy asked, always the humanitarian. "Can you bring our missing crew back to life?"

"No. Reassembling dead matter is easy, but life is a complex material. Once it has been extinguished, it cannot be reassembled."

Everybody watched as the ship docked on the beach. It looked magnificent and brand new. The captain ran up to his precious vessel and did his best to hug it.

"We're going home!" the captain exulted.

Brody's spirits sank as he accepted the weight the moment had for him. This was the moment he had dreaded. He looked at Rose to examine her reaction. She appeared sanguine. It didn't make sense, so Brody turned to Benedict. Benedict's expression was resistant to Brody's stare.

"She doesn't know, does she?" Brody adroitly surmised.

Benedict sighed and looked guilty. "She won't let you go. I couldn't tell her that you have to leave. She won't stand for it."

Brody looked to Adam in the hope that he might have a modicum of humanity. "Benedict's right," he asserted. "Rose and I have to be together. None of this is her fault. Let me stay for her sake."

"The conditions for your continuation on this island were made clear. The individual known as Edmund must cease to exist as a compromise. If you are not willing to sanction his negation, then you must leave, or the consequences will be dire for all of your party."

Everybody felt bad. Nobody wanted to sacrifice themselves or their friends for the sake of one love affair. Least of all Brody, who didn't have the psychopathy to betray his friends even for the love of his life. Brody gave a final, pleading look towards Benedict for his assistance. Benedict gave a strong facial indication that he was powerless to help.

"Tell her," Brody insisted. "Tell her the truth this time."

In her heart, Rose knew what was going on, but she was relying on the comfort of denial to protect her from facing it. Benedict placed her face in his hands and made her look at him. Rose trusted Benedict essentially, but she was resistant to see what he had to show her. Benedict looked over at Brody to warn him that what was about happen wasn't going to be pleasant, and then he conveyed to her the truth about Brody's impending departure.

The flurry of Rose's fury surprised nobody but shocked everyone. She screeched a primordial rage that ate at the souls of every witness. She punched Benedict to extricate a lie she needed to hear. His pictures couldn't be true. His pictures in her mind *couldn't* be true. The crowd reacted with ambivalent certainty. None of them could stomach the scene of Rose's heartbreak, and all of them couldn't do a thing to prevent it. Rose became an animal in light of the information Benedict had imparted, and she shot cursing glares at everybody around her. The only person she didn't execute with her eyes was Brody, who she respected and forgave unconditionally. The forgiveness she extended was borne from her understanding of his decision to save his friends. She loved him for that, but she still wasn't willing to let him go. Once she had condemned everybody with her eyes, she turned again to Benedict to ask him with mental pictures if there was a way for her to stay with him. Benedict told her that Brody could be with her if Edmund died. To Rose, this was a simple solution, an obvious resolution and she lunged at Edmund without any initial hint of conscience. Edmund knew what was at stake. *He* was at stake, for the sake of Rose and Brody. Edmund didn't resist.

"Leave him alone," Condy screamed.

Rose's fury was absolute.

Edmund fixed his eyes on Rose and didn't struggle. He didn't say anything. Rose looked into his eyes and saw that he was complicit with her determination. She hesitated, looking to Brody for his advocacy. Brody shook his head to indicate to Rose that her intended action was not warrantable, which indicated to Rose that she should cease her murderous instinct and diminish her violent response. So, instead of fighting, Rose took to screaming as harshly as she could to express how much she fiercely objected to Benedict's insistence that she must accept Brody's departure. She ran over the Benedict once again and asked in his head if she could go with Brody. Benedict said that Adam wouldn't allow it. Rose lunged at Adam and beat him as hard as she could with her fists and her feet. Adam couldn't be harmed, and he withstood the attack calmly. After a few seconds of Rose's futile attack, Brody approached her from behind, gently putting both his hands on her arms. Rose flinched at first but then she sensed it was Brody and simply turned and plunged herself into his arms, sobbing wildly into his chest.

"Come on everybody," the captain said during this relative calm. "Let's get on board."

Rose clung onto Brody with her entire strength. Brody clung back. He thought maybe if they just held onto each other, everyone would go away and let them be. It was an optimistic thought, but it was the only hope he had left.

Most of the crew started to make their way aboard the ship. Condy and Edmund boarded together, looking back at Brody and Rose the whole time. Zachary and the captain realised that someone had to separate the two lovers and get Brody on board, so they volunteered to make the attempt. Mrs. LaGrance and Bridie stood by the ship and watched. As Zachary and the captain approached Brody and Rose still embracing, Brody sensed them coming.

"Stay Back!" he demanded.

"Brody, you have to come with us," the captain insisted.

"I can't leave her!" Brody cried. "I'll hate you all forever if you take me away from her."

"Oh, grow up, Brody!" Zachary blasted. "You're acting like a teenager with his first crush."

"But that's exactly what it's like," Brody replied. "It's like every love affair I've had until now was a rehearsal for the real thing, and now it's hit me like an unstoppable force. I didn't understand love before I met Rose, and now I can't go back. There's no way I can go back."

Bridie began to cry on hearing Brody's words. She was crying for two reasons. Firstly, she was empathetic to the plight of the tragic lovers, and secondly, she was upset for herself that Brody was effectively saying he never loved her as much as he was in love with Rose.

Brody could hear Bridie crying, not far away. Still holding onto Rose and not turning to look at Bridic, he spoke to her. "Bridie. I'm sorry if that upsets you. When I say love, I mean romantic love. I never felt it so strong before."

"And that's supposed to make me feel better?"

"You're my best friend. You always have been. I love you platonically more than I have ever loved anyone platonically, and I always will."

"Stop trying to placate me. If you feel guilty… Good!" Bridie emotionally poured. "All you care about is your new girlfriend."

"My wife!" he corrected. "And it's not true. I care about you, too. I'm going to prove it to you now."

"How?" Bridie asked.

Brody didn't answer in words, he simply leaned back a little from Rose and gently, gently, gently pushed her from his chest. Rose looked up at him, with her big red eyes, red from the tears, and she waited to see what he would do next. Brody leaned in and kissed her lips. Rose returned the kiss not knowing that it was his goodbye kiss. Brody began to cry. Just a few dribbling tears that he had failed to keep back. As the tender kiss ended, and they leaned away from each other, Rose could see the new tears on Brody's face, but before she had time to interpret why he was crying, Benedict and Adam appeared behind her, taking her arms in restraint. Brody let go of Rose's hands but didn't take his eyes off her. Rose panicked and screamed and struggled to free herself from the grip of the immortals. It was a task she couldn't master, but she gave it a damn good try. She pulled and swung herself, kicked and screamed and flailed in a desperate plea to escape, but Benedict and Adam were too strong. Zachary put a friendly hand on Brody's shoulder as an offer to lead him to the ship. Brody, still fixed on Rose's eyes and sporting a new expression of tears, slowly began stepping backwards towards the ship. Rose was still fighting and struggling to free herself, but she was now doing it to a chorus of gurgles as she screamed out and wept at the same time. Brody continued to retreat to the boat, with his eyes locked on Rose's. He started to babble his apology to her just with his eyes until, with Zachary and the captain's assistance, he reached the ship.

By now, Rose knew that Brody was leaving her. She understood why, she didn't blame him. Rose knew that he didn't want to leave her, but that he had to protect his people, and she wasn't going to let him go without a fight. Her outrage was tangible. She wouldn't stop protesting until Brody was gone. She dug her nails into Benedict's flesh and her fury was enough to scratch away at Adam's skin. Adam flinched at her clawing because it was the first time he had ever been hurt. As an immortal, he couldn't rationally be hurt, but Rose's love for Brody and her resistance to losing him had made it possible. It was an event which caused Adam to respect and fear the sheer power that unbridled love could inflict.

Brody snivelled with retched maudlin as he boarded the ship. He was a mess. His attempts to be brave were easily quashed by the certainty of a future without Rose. Each step he took on board cut at his heart until he couldn't even stand anymore. Zachary and the captain had to hold him up and drag him onto the ship. Brody slumped on the deck and wept, a pathetic, sorry, self-indulgent corpse of a man. Rose stamped on Benedict's feet and pulled at Adam's hair in a gambit to free herself. Her scourge of fury caused her two captors to let go of her and she scampered into the water to get as close to Brody as she could. But it was too late. The ship was heading out. Rose hurried into the water up to her neck and she watched as the ship housing her husband sailed away from her. Rose, like all the muties, didn't know how to swim. It was a skill they hadn't had any reason to master, so none of them had ever bothered to learn. Brody crawled exhaustedly to the stern of the ship and he hung over the edge watching the love of his life become more distant as the ship ferried away from the island.

Despite her inability to swim, Rose carried on into the ocean, becoming immersed in the water. Benedict wasn't going to let her drown, and he plunged into the sea, pulling her back to the shallows, saving her life. Rose protested by splashing and giving force against Benedict, but Benedict was determined to see her survive. Rose resisted because she felt that she would rather die than see Brody go. Benedict wasn't going to let her die.

Bridie and Condy and several others on the ship watched the spectacle of Brody and Rose's devotion to each other and they couldn't bear it. Those who had a penchant for tears were indulgent and many of the others who were generally more stoical couldn't help themselves either. As the ship disappeared into the shroud of fog encircling the island, the last thing they all heard were the unstifled cries of Rose's anguish. If there was any consolation for Brody and Rose, it was that their hearts broke at the same moment.

## CHAPTER TWELVE
## "HENRY"

Brody lay on the stern of the ship, refusing to move and attempting not to breath. The stark, crushing reality of never seeing Rose again was more than he was willing to bear, and he foolishly tried to auto-suffocate. It wasn't possible of course. He couldn't even make himself pass out. He tried slamming his head onto the deck of the ship to knock himself out but each time he did it just made him weaker and less able to bang his head so hard. Bridie watched in horror at first and then she came to her senses and ran over to be there for her best friend. The ship was now cruising across the water, and the island had been lost in the fog.

"Brody," she said softly. "Brody, honey."

Brody remained face down on the deck, breathing heavily through the tears and snot.

Bridie knelt down next to him and put her hands on his shoulders affectionately. "Brody, listen to me please," she began, but he didn't give her chance to continue.

"What?" he asked furiously. "Are you going to tell me that I'll get over her? Are you gonna say it'll get easier, that I'll learn to deal with it?" he fumed, still pushing his face into the wooden floor.

"No," Bridie replied. "I was going to tell you that I've never seen two people more broken up by being separated before," she said. "I wanted to tell you that I wish I loved someone so much that I would literally rather die than lose them. I wish I knew what that felt like. At the same time, I don't envy you. I don't envy how you must feel now… now that you've lost everything."

Brody just breathed noisily for a few moments and then he made the painful move from being on his front to sitting up right next to Bridie. He looked into his best friend's beautiful, glowing, sensitive face and made his best effort to smile. It didn't go well, so he put his hand on Bridie's cheek to let her know he appreciated her words. "I haven't lost *everything*," he told her.

Bridie tried to smile and was somewhat more successful at it than Brody had been. Their touching moment was rudely interrupted by the distinct, unmistakable sound of the roar of the T-Rex not far off. The whole crew turned their eyes in search of the T-Rex. For Brody, this was the first time he had heard the roar of the dinosaur.

"Was that the T-Rex?" he asked Bridie.

"Yep, that's Henry," she confirmed.

"It sounds just like the T-Rex in Jurassic Park."

"I know. Isn't that cool?"

Brody just looked confused. "But it doesn't make sense. When they made Jurassic Park, they had no idea what dinosaurs sounded like, so they had to create the sounds using their imaginations and combining the sounds of modern animals. It's a complete fabrication."

Bridie's face twisted in confusion as Brody spoke. "You're right. It doesn't make sense."

"Meaning that it's an astonishing coincidence, or this T-Rex is was designed after the fact of Jurassic Park, using the movie as a template."

"Or that this T-Rex is mimicking the movie," Bridie suggested.

"Either way, it's an anachronism."

"Pretty much."

The T-Rex roared again. This time it was distinctly closer. The crew of the ship, all standing on the deck, looked out into the surrounding fog to see if they could spot any sign of the T-Rex.

"Look!" one of the as-yet unnamed crew screamed. Everybody looked at the crewman in order to see where he was looking, and then they all looked at what he was looking at. He was looking at the T-Rex, slowly emerging from the fog. Henry didn't look happy.

Brody, who hadn't seen the T-Rex before, took a few fascinated steps towards the dinosaur, racked with wonder. "That's incredible!"

"That's Henry," Bridie said.

Brody managed to take his gaze from the T-rex to shoot a look at Bridie. "You said he can talk, right?"

"Yeah. But he doesn't look like he came here for a chat!"

"On the contrary," boomed the T-Rex having to increase his volume to talk over his own tidal wave splashing. "I have something very important to say."

Everybody stared at the T-Rex waiting for him to continue talking. The T-Rex stopped moving and waited for the waves to die down leaving him standing in the water, staring at the entire crew of the ship on the deck. A strange silence fell littered only with the sound of the calm ocean. The T-Rex looked over all the faces of the humans and there was one he didn't recognise.

"You must be Brody," he said.

Brody nervously cleared his throat. "Yes, and you must be Henry."

"No, I'm the other unique, immortal dinosaur of Mesaglenedendeltor," Henry replied sarcastically.

"What do you want, Henry?" Condy asked, afraid that she knew the answer.

"When you crossed the island," Henry began, "I allowed you to pass the barrier on the condition, Condy, that you would later make a sacrifice."

Everybody froze as they realised what was going on. Edmund took hold of Condy's hand and looked into her eyes.

"We thought, from what Adam said, that we had a choice," Condy replied with hope.

The T-Rex sighed. "I'm afraid Adam misled you. The sacrifice is still owed, and if Edmund does not give his life willingly, I am afraid I will have to extinguish you all," the T-Rex revealed gravely. "Sorry, everyone, but those are the rules."

Edmund didn't take his eyes off Condy. "Condy," he said gently.

"No."

"Condy, let me do this."

"No."

"This time, it's not just for Brody and Rose. This time, it's to save your life."

"No! I've told you no, and I'm still saying no."

Edmund flashed a look across at Zachary and the captain who realised that their restraining duties were necessary again. The two men sidled surreptitiously over towards Condy.

Brody watched the spectacle with ambiguous certainty that he should step in and that they all should make a stand. He strode over to Condy and Edmund, watching the T-Rex as he did so. "Mr. T-Rex!" he cried out. "I'm afraid we are going to have to refuse."

"Brody, what are you doing?" Edmund asked furiously.

Brody turned to Edmund, his facial expression determined and grave. "These immortals keep threatening us but none of them have harmed us. In fact, Julianne saved us all from the water when we arrived. I don't think the T-Rex will harm us."

"That's a hell of a risk, Brody," Zachary said as he and the captain joined the conversation.

"I'm with Brody," Condy quickly chimed.

"As Captain, I'm in favour of any action that protects my passengers – every one of them."

Edmund darted his eyes from face to face until all the faces were spent. The final face he rested on was Condy's. Her eyes seemed so desperate for him to live, that Edmund found himself wavering, and he couldn't fool himself that it wasn't a relief to consider the idea of living. "I'm not sure…" he began

"Listen to me," Condy screamed at him with conviction. "You're coming with me, inside the ship and we're going to leave these waters, all of us, and return to England where you and me are going to build a life together. Do you understand?"

"Shouldn't that be you and I?" Zachary said.

"Grow up!" Condy replied, and then she grabbed Edmund's hand and led him doggedly inside the ship.

Everybody watched this happen and then turned to look at the T-Rex who was eerily motionless as he watched Edmund being taken away. One by one, the passengers of the ship, followed Condy and Edmund inside the apparent safety of the ship. The last to leave was Brody, who continued to watch the T-Rex. "We're calling your bluff," he cried out just before he went inside, leaving the deck of the ship abandoned.

Inside, everybody piled onto the bridge and some of the crew began trying to navigate the ship around the T-Rex. In the short time it had taken them to reach the bridge, the weather seemed to have significantly worsened. Waves were crashing and the rain poured down like a monsoon. The ship swayed from side to side to up to down causing many of the passengers and crew to fall to the floor. There was commotion, panic and a lot of inarticulate shouting going on. Condy held tightly onto Edmund who was preoccupied with the guilt that by protecting him, they were all putting their lives in danger. Edmund had wanted so badly to live, that he had let everybody convince him that they could all survive without his sacrifice.

Outside, the T-Rex let out an almighty roar that shattered all the glass on the bridge of the ship and struck terror into everybody on board. With the windows gone, everybody was exposed to the ferocious weather conditions. The stabbing rain and disorienting wind tore at everybody no matter where they tried to hide, and waves crashed in from the ocean. It was difficult for anybody to see anything through the sheets of rain everywhere they turned. The crew had no chance of navigating the ship in any way. The captain held desperately onto his seafaring instruments but he couldn't operate them.

"It's no good!" the captain cried, his voice barely being audible, drowned out by the sea and weather. "We can't navigate in this, and it won't be long until the ship goes down."

As if to concur with the captain's appraisal, the T-Rex roared viciously once again.

Edmund made his ultimate, noble and damning decision. He staggered to his feet and felt his way round the edge of the room to peer out of the shattered window. Condy, aware of what he was trying to do, tried her best to stay with him, but she was thrown to the floor by the waves, rain and wind. Edmund managed to stay on his feet. Once he could see the T-Rex, he waved his arms in the air in the hope of getting the dinosaur's attention. The T-Rex seemed to notice.

"Hey!" Edmund screamed at Henry.

The commotion suddenly ceased. The boat rocked one final time and then became level. The rain reduced to a light shower, the wind to a gentle breeze, and the waves waved goodbye.

"Yes, Edmund?" Henry asked.

Edmund crawled carefully out through the smashed bridge window and back onto the deck of the ship. Close behind him was Condy and the others all followed once they got their breaths back.

"I'm ready now. I know there's no way round it. Spare my friends."

Condy caught up with Edmund and she took hold of his arm with both of hers. Edmund turned to look into her eyes. Her eyes were full of heartache.

"Don't try to stop me this time," Edmund pleaded.

Condy didn't reply immediately. She was reluctant to say what she knew she had to say. It had become clear during the storm that either Edmund had to die, or they all had to die. "Okay," she simply, sadly said.

Edmund was pleased that she was finally on board with what had to happen, but also found himself a little upset that she had stopped fighting against his death. He decided it was best to shield her from this. "Thankyou," he said. He leaned in tentatively to kiss her, and Condy grabbed hold of his face and pulled herself in to snog his breath away. When she eventually let him get his breath back, Edmund turned to look at Henry again, firmly clutching Condy's hand.

"How do we do this?" Edmund nervously asked. "Are you going to eat me?"

"Urgh!" the T-Rex wretched. "I'm not going to eat you. I'm a vegan."

Henry's claim caused everybody to freeze. Some of them let out a nervous laugh.

"Tyrannosaurs are carnivores," Bridie exclaimed. "How can you be vegan?"

Henry snorted. "Humans are carnivores, and some of you are vegan," he argued simplistically.

Nobody could fault this logic.

“So, what, then? Are you going to tear me apart with your talons or claws or whatever they are?”

“Claws,” Bridie clarified.

The T-Rex slowly shook his big head. “It’s Condy’s sacrifice. She has to do it,” he revealed.

“What? No,” Condy blurted desperately.

Edmund took hold of Condy’s shoulders and poured his soul deep into her eyes. He didn’t say anything at first, he just looked at her in a way that told Condy that he expected that she could kill him. “You can save your friends,” he said eventually.

“By killing you?”

“You can do it. You have my permission,” he told her confidently. “You have my blessing.”

Condy knew what she had to do, but she wasn’t willing. She turned her attention to Henry. “Why does it have to be me?”

The T-Rex growled out of impatience and leaned closer to the ship. “Because it isn’t a sacrifice if you don’t do it.”

Condy understood, but even if she accepted her fate and Edmund’s she didn’t think she was emotionally capable of murder. She focussed on Edmund. “I don’t think I can kill you.”

Condy felt something cold and metallic touch her arm. When she looked down to see what it was, she realised the captain was handing her a firearm. She refused to take it, so Edmund took the weapon from the captain and pressed it gently into Condy’s hands. He then pressed the barrel of the gun to his forehead with Condy’s hands still attached. Condy was staggered by how brave Edmund was being about his impending death. She wished she had the same courage. Condy stepped back from Edmund, not to get away from him, but it was an instinctive way to move the gun further from him, as if shooting him from a few feet further away would somehow be less lethal. Condy froze and shook at the same time. Her fear had petrified her and she was absolutely unable to take any action.

"Get on with it!" Henry boomed at her.

Condy erupted into tears, lowering the gun slightly.

"Leave her alone!" Edmund demanded, and he stepped forward and lifted Condy's arms and the gun back into position.

"I can't do this," she squeaked.

"Look at it this way… if you take my life, then my life belongs to you, and I'll be with you for ever."

"I'll never get over it," Condy said sadly.

"It'll make you stronger," Edmund replied. "Would you grant me a last request?"

"Anything," Condy agreed eagerly.

"Dump your arsehole boyfriend."

Condy made a sort of smile. "Definitely," she promised.

On the tail of her reply, the increasingly impatient T-Rex let out a frustrated and deafening roar which set the tides waving again and caused Condy's trigger finger to squeeze reactively. The gun went off. Edmund dropped to the deck, blood gushing from a new hole in his head. Condy dropped the gun and, weak with remorse, fell to her knees and then down onto her side where she wept loudly. Everybody else was in shock. The new waves slowly calmed and became still. Henry, satisfied with the situation, simply and unceremoniously turned and walked through the ocean back towards his island.

Brody and Bridie dashed over to Condy's side to comfort her as much as they could. Bridie put her hands on Condy's shoulder, kneeling beside her, and Brody took one of her hands in both of his. Condy continued to scream and cry mournfully. Behind her, Zachary and the captain attended to the duty of taking Edmund's body indoors to be stored for burial. Both Brody and Bridie were racking their minds for something appropriate to say. Neither of them succeeded. The situation remained unchanged for a few minutes. Condy's exhaustive crying lessened slowly until she reached a point of only incessant sobbing. Finally, she moved from her position on her side, to be sitting upright. She tilted her head and looked at Brody. Her eyes were bloodshot and broken and her surrounding skin was wrinkled, pink and wet. Brody finally managed to say something.

"I'm so sorry, Condy," he weakly condoled.

Condy let go of his hands and put her hands on his cheeks. Her eyes had turned fierce. "Go to your wife," she said with ferocious passion.

Brody didn't reply. He was confused at first, but through the fog of confusion, he began to realise what she was saying.

"Edmund's dead," Condy elaborated morosely. "Adam said you could stay with Rose once Edmund was dead."

Brody's tears come through. He was genuinely sorry for Edmund's death, but he was mostly crying because of Condy's incredible humanity at thinking of him at possibly the worst moment of her life.

"Go and be with Rose. Go and make her happy. Make Edmund's death worth it."

Brody brushed Condy's hair from her face and kissed her on the forehead. "Thank you," he said softly before getting to his feet and looking out at the ocean behind them. He could still see the shore. He could swim it. Brody looked around at his friends and colleagues. Each one of them as he saw their eyes nodded or smiled in a gesture of approval and encouragement. All except Bridie, who Brody deliberately looked to last, knowing that saying goodbye to her was going to be nearly as hard as saying goodbye to Rose had been.

Bridie was standing now, looking at her feet, avoiding Brody's eye contact. Brody took one step to be close enough to her to lift her head up with his hand. As he did this, she darted her eyes to the left which made Brody smile. He took both her hands in his. She didn't resist.

"Look at me?" he asked.

"No," Bridie said.

"Will you look at me, please. I want to tell you I love you before I go and I'm not going to say it until you look at me."

Bridie took a deep breath in and then relented and looked into Brody's eyes. She welled up a little bit but remained in control.

"I love you," Brody said earnestly.

"Okay," she replied with embittered dismissiveness.

Brody waited a moment. "Aren't you going to tell me…?"

"No," she interrupted. "I don't want you to go."

"I know. The thought of never seeing you again hurts me more than I can tell you, but…"

"You have to be with your wife. I get it. I'm being selfish."

"Yes, you are," Brody joked.

Bridie couldn't help but smile. Brody kissed her on the nose which made her smile a little wider, and then Brody let go of her hands and ran to the edge of the deck. He stepped up and held onto the taffrail as though he was about to climb over and dive in the water. He looked down into the cold ocean and had a moment's doubt, but then he pictured Rose in his mind and all his doubts drowned. He turned and looked at Bridie who was reluctantly anticipating his departure.

"I'm going," Brody teased her. "It's your last chance to tell me you love me."

Bridie sighed and almost gave in to his charm. "No. I'm angry with you."

"Because…?" Brody followed.

"Because I love you and I don't want you to go," she finally admitted.

Brody smiled. "I wish you could come with me, but I don't think Adam would allow it."

"I couldn't stay here anyway," Bridie replied. "One of us needs to continue our work."

Brody nodded and took in a deep breath in acceptance of the fact it was almost time for him to go. He looked around the deck at everybody once more. They all looked sad and happy, but none of them were discouraging about Brody's decision. "I'm going to miss all of you," Brody said affectionately, and he saved his last words for Bridie. "And I'll miss you most of all, Scarecrow!"

Bridie giggled at Brody's multi-layered movie quote. "Is that The Wizard of Oz or…?"

"I was thinking Top Secret."

"Have you realised that when you go, you'll never see another movie again?"

Brody stammered slightly at this realisation. "Oh my God!" he exclaimed. "That means the last movie I will ever have seen is Beverly Hills Chihuahua 3!"

Everybody laughed at this, most of all Bridie. Even Condy managed to chortle between her sobs.

Brody looked down into the ocean once more. "Bridie, honey, if you're ever in the neighbourhood…"

Bridie smiled. "I'll pop in," she said.

And then Brody was gone. He stepped over the taffrail and leapt into the cold ocean. Brodie and some of the others ran to the edge of the boat to see if he was alright. The drop hadn't been too far, and they could clearly see Brody swimming away from them in the now calm waters.

# CHAPTER THIRTEEN
# "THE END"

Rose was still standing in the water. She had watched the ship take her Brody away and she hadn't taken her eyes off it. She had screamed and cried when she had seen the T-Rex approach the ship and she had coughed with fury at Henry when he appeared to be attacking the ship. And then when she had seen Henry returning to the island leaving the ship still intact, she had calmed down a little but she was still suffering the intensity of absolute loss. As Henry had reached the shore and plodded over the beach straight past Rose, she had virtually ignored him to continue watching the ship which was only just still visible through the mist. Rose continued to stare at the ship until, only minutes later, it was engulfed in the fog and she could no longer see where it had gone. Her desperate eyes peered into the fog as if she could will the fog away and get a clear view of the departing ship. She was also picturing the ship in her head and it was turning around and coming to bring Brody back to her… in her head. Rose knew that the immortals had the power to move things with pictures in their heads so she saw no reason why she wouldn't be able to master the skill in this extreme circumstance. The ship didn't turn around, but as she stared into the distance, she started to make out a singular movement, a splashing movement, happening just underneath the fog-line. Her hand went to her mouth and her stomach leapt into her throat as she imagined that her hope to be reunited with Brody could now be happening. Rose edged to the left and to the right, jittery at the uncertainty of what she was seeing in the distance. She splashed her arms excitedly in the water and yelped with anticipation because she didn't have the will to doubt it could be Brody.

The immortals on the beach, who had been watching Rose since the ship had left and who had all been shocked and confused by her heartbreak, took notice of her new excitable behaviour. They moved down the beach towards the shore.

Rose was going mental now. Screaming joyously and slamming her arms onto the surface of the water to make the loudest splash sounds she could make. Her underused voice went through a range of squeaks and yelps and giggles as she watched the thing in the water come closer to her. Even though she couldn't even see if the emerging splasher was human, she absolutely knew it was Brody coming back for her.

The immortals, one by one, looked out at the ocean to see if they could see what Rose had become so excited about. Benedict was the first to notice the splashing thing in the distance. "There, look!" he said, pointing.

The other immortals followed the line of Benedict's pointing finger until they could see it too.

"What's that?" Julianne asked.

"You mean *who's* that?" Adam corrected, knowing very well what was happening.

The penny dropped for Benedict, Julianne and Sabrina at Adam's comment.

"Henry demanded his sacrifice," Sabrina said.

"Which means Edmund died," Julianne continued.

Adam sighed. "Which means, the terms of Brody's return have been met," he concluded.

Benedict said nothing. He just smiled with relief that Rose would get the man she loved back. Benedict hadn't been enjoying the thought of attempting to nurse her broken heart, and now it wouldn't be necessary.

Rose could now make out the splashing figure enough to know it was human. She became even more excited and she wished she knew how to swim so she could go and greet him sooner. She waded as far in as she could, until the water was at her neckline and she continued to watch the swimming man approach her.

Brody was running out of energy. He estimated he was about half-way to the beach and he didn't know if he had the strength to make it all the way. He would have to stop for a moment and catch his breath. He managed to keep above the surface while he took his break from the swim and got his breathing under control.

"You can do it, Brody," he heard a familiar voice say.

Brody turned his head sharply to see Iain, the ship's psychiatrist in the water beside him. "Iain?"

"Don't worry, I'm just a temporary hallucination brought on by recent general stress, heartache and your exertion in the water. I'll go away in a minute,"

"Okay. Good."

"While I'm here, I need to tell you how glad I am that you managed to find your way back to Rose again," Iain said with a tone in his voice that indicated there was something contextual hidden in what he was saying.

Brody smiled. "From the moment I met her, it was as though we had always been together," he said with melodramatic sentiment. "It sounds silly, but it feels right."

"It doesn't sound silly at all," Iain claimed. "I had no doubt you could do it again,"

Brody frowned. "What do you mean?" he asked, but the hallucination of Iain was gone. Brody looked all around, but there was no sign of the imaginary psychiatrist. Brody decided to dismiss the momentary distraction and concentrate on the important task of reaching Rose. He could see the beach fairly clearly now and it wasn't long before he saw Rose's head and shoulders jutting out of the water near the shoreline. Brody's heart began to race and he flung his arm high out of the water to signal to her. In the distance, he watched her replicate his action, and she waved her arm in the air. This was the motivation Brody needed and he immediate resumed swimming towards the beach. Knowing she was waiting for him and that he couldn't bear to wait a second longer than he had to before holding her again, Brody swam with unrelenting speed and boundless energy.

Having had absolute confirmation that the swimming body was indeed Brody, Rose was going bananas at expressing her joy with flailing arms and exuberant primeval cries. Before long Brody was close enough for them to hear each other.

"Rose!" he cried out the best that he could despite the water impeding his speech.

Rose simply screamed a sustained song of delight at the return of her husband, keeping her head well above the water in order for her voice to be pure. Brody listened to her sweet aria and thought it was the most beautiful thing he had ever heard.

And when Brody arrived in Rose's vicinity, he was so excited and eager to get to her he almost smacked her in the face with his splashing, swimming arms. Rose put her own arms out to defend herself from the unintended attack and within seconds they were holding each other with such unrestrained force that they almost did each other damage. Brody pulled back a little for the sake of his health and for the sake of looking at Rose's gorgeous eyes again. They gazed at each other for a few seconds and then kissed with maritime marital eternity until they absolutely had to come up for breath. And then they returned to gazing again, neither of them feeling moved enough to get out of the water. What surrounded them meant nothing for the moment. Only that they were together mattered. Brody wanted to tell Rose that he was staying with her forever, but he wasn't sure how to make her understand, and then he remembered something. Brody held up one of his fingers, pointed to himself with it and held it up again to symbolise 'one'. He then put two of his fingers together to make a plus symbol and followed this with another single finger representing 'one' again. He pointed the finger at Rose this time and then did his best to signify ‘equals’ with two fingers. Rose smiled, pushed his hands away and, with her other hand, extended her index finger to symbolise ‘one’.

“One plus one equals one,” Brody said to confirm it to himself.

They didn’t need speech to communicate. They were perfectly synchronised. Rose and Brody walked back to the beach, kissed, and consummated their marriage yet again.

Printed in Great Britain
by Amazon